Thirst

By the same author

Brahma's Dream

Awake When All the World is Asleep

Thirst

Shree Ghatage

Doubleday Canada

Doubleday Canada and colophon are registered trademarks

Library and Archives Canada Cataloguing in Publication

Ghatage, Shree
        Thirst / Shree Ghatage.

Issued also in electronic format.
ISBN 978-0-385-66665-7

        I. Title.

PS8563.H37T47 2012   C813'.54   C2011-908488-0

This book is a work of fiction. Names, characters, places and incidents are products of the author's imagination or are used fictitiously. Any resemblance to actual events or locales or persons, living or dead, is entirely coincidental.

Cover and text design: Leah Springate
Cover images: (room) Dan Duchars/ GAP Photos/Getty Images, (Big Ben) Valueline/Punchstock, (frame) © Pictac | Dreamstime.com, (texture) Shutterstock.com
Printed and bound in the USA

Published in Canada by Doubleday Canada, a division of Random House of Canada Limited

www.randomhouse.ca

10 9 8 7 6 5 4 3 2 1

XCIV

Should I die, survive me with a force so pure
That you awaken fury from the pale, chill world,
In all directions raise your indelible eyes,
Day in, day out, sound your mouth's guitar.

I don't want your footsteps to vacillate
Nor your smile wane, I don't want my bequeathed joy
To die. Don't come knocking at my chest, I'm away.
Dwell in my absence as you would in my estate.

Absence is such a vast house
That you will walk through its walls
And hang paintings in the air.

Absence is such a transparent house
That without my own life I will watch you live
And if I see you suffer, my love, I will die again.

One Hundred Love Sonnets, PABLO NERUDA
(translated by Rafael Campo)

London

August 4, 1942

My darling Vasanti,

I don't believe there was a moment during those long days
and nights on the ship when I stopped thinking about you.
Every time I saw a golden moon rising on the horizon, I
would think: My Vasanti would have thrilled at the sight
of this. At night, when the Americans who were travelling
with me brought out their musical instruments and sang
their beautiful songs, I wished you could have heard them,
especially the astonishing eight-year-old boy playing the
banjo as though he had learned it inside his mother's womb.
But in that last week before we reached Liverpool the seas
were treacherous, and one of the ship's officers told me
that the Captain was getting navigational instructions
hourly from central command. I was glad then that you
were not with me.

London is not as cold as I expected it to be, but it is only my third day here. Yesterday I went to Christopher's house, and to my utter surprise his sister opened the door. We didn't get much of a chance to catch up but I'm planning to have them over for tea one day soon.

Yesterday I also walked around the city for several hours. I went past the magnificent buildings of the Palace of Westminster where the wartime cabinet sits. Big Ben, the tallest, most accurate clock in the world, would have impressed you. I saw from the outside Westminster Abbey where King George VI and Her Royal Highness Queen Elizabeth were married.

You are not to worry about me, Vasanti. I insist upon that. As you know, it is several months since the Nazi bombs fell, and when you see Londoners go about their business in a purposeful fashion, watch young children play hop-scotch and skip rope, and visit the abundant gardens and squares adorned by summer blossoms, the war on the continent seems far away. So don't be anxious on my account and continue to live in the knowledge that I am faring well. I did a lot of thinking on my way here, and I want you to know that as soon as I am finished my studies I will return to you and our life together— I promise. I don't want you to fret and think that I abandoned you by choosing to leave for England when I did. That is simply not the case, as you will one day find out. I will look into your eyes and tell you stories about my adventures and satisfy that endearing curiosity of yours that I have come to love so well.

I want you to eat, sleep and study hard. And I want you to continue to coach badminton in the hope that one day, at least one of your pupils—my uncoordinated sisters-in-law—will be able to challenge you to a decent game! Give my regards to them and everyone back home, and please also include my greetings to your aunts and your family in Bombay. And continue to pray for us both at the temple each morning.

Write back to me as soon as you receive this letter and give me all your news. Leave nothing out. I want you to know that I will start looking for your reply exactly eight weeks from now, the time I think it will take for our missives to crisscross the oceans. I miss you more and more each day, my dear dear love.

With lots and lots of kisses,
Only yours forever and always,
Baba

I

August 1942

Nᴏʀᴛʜ Wᴀʟᴇs ᴀɴᴅ Lᴏɴᴅᴏɴ, UK

~ ONE ~

H E COMES AWAKE TO A steady drumming and opens his eyes; rain is battering the windowpane and the austere light is so diffuse that he wonders if he is going blind. The chill has penetrated his body and turned it into a jagged ball of ice. He pulls up the scratchy blanket to cover his neck, and swallows several times in an attempt to moisten his throat. Eyes adjusting to the dimness, he takes in the scarred cupboard, the yellow-centred daisies in the blue porcelain vase, the patchwork cushion propped against the wall. Recognizing nothing, he turns towards the ceiling. At once, the rear of his skull feels hit by a mallet. He recoils onto his side and whimpers in pain.

Immediately, as though waiting in the adjacent room for just such a sign of wakefulness, a balding man with a flattened boxer's face opens the door, his gumboots releasing into the air a dank odour of rubber. Mr. Owens. Standing by the bed he leans over and examines the huddled man's head. "The swelling is somewhat reduced," he says, "which means my ointment has worked."

The wounded man tries to sit up in bed. Propping himself on his elbows, he opens his mouth to speak. What issues is an incoherent whisper. Embarrassed, he steeples his palms and fingers together in a gesture of gratitude.

"Think nothing of it," Mr. Owens says; his eyes are a clear, kind blue, with pink around the edges. He places his hand on the man's forehead and says, "Your body is still on fire. Another fever cordial is what you need." He exits the room, only to return after a few minutes, one hand holding a lemon-coloured drink, the other a plate on which sits a thick slice of bread sparsely covered with butter.

The wounded man eats the bread quickly, and after he has mopped up the crumbs with his fingers, wets his throat with the cordial. He glances around the room, a question in his eyes.

But his host is in a hurry to leave. "Rest now," Mr. Owens says, "and keep faith that by the time I return this evening, your memory will have too."

Upon hearing a door shut, and soon after, the creaking of a gate, the man sits up gingerly. Shrugging out of his borrowed pyjamas, he reaches for the clothes on the chair next to him. He slips into them, but no sooner has he placed his feet on the floor than the room begins to spin. Filled with agitation, he lies down again and tosses and turns on his narrow bed, the refrain of *who am I* a drumbeat reverberating through his body. At long last, to the chimes of distant church bells, he falls asleep.

It is still light outside when the sound of music coaxes him awake. Someone is playing the piano. All at once becalmed, he listens to the melody, and no sooner is his mind diverted by its clear haunting echo than it stops mid-phrase and the air is pricked by sharp needles of silence. Just as he is wondering whether he should call out to the old man who has looked after him so well, the unseen hands start once again to play. This time loud notes are banged out in descending order and the man on the bed flinches in pain. There is the sharp scrape of a stool followed by the rustle of pages. Deft hands begin a new composition; languid at first, the music soon surges and as it expands and fills the air, the man shuffles to the door and opens it a slit.

A paraffin lamp throws light on a young woman who is seated at the piano, her back turned to him. She continues to play with one hand while straightening the score sheet with the other, and says to someone he cannot see, "How about this?" She runs her hands up and down the length of the keys, her fingers leading her body, her foot keeping pace with the tempo. Addressing another person, this time to her right, she mutters, "Did you not hear?" And before anyone can answer, she slams shut the lid of the piano and slides her legs over its bench, facing him. Her skin is coarse and uneven, her hair a chestnut brown. Bending down, she pulls up a bunched sock and her single plait falls forward and brackets one side of her face. The man standing behind the partially open door, a voyeur in a life he cannot yet identify is momentarily stirred into a flash of sweet memory.

Without looking his way, the woman smoothes her smock and moves out of sight, showing him a silhouette that is bony and girlish, pitifully so. He hears the sound of a pot being stirred and an aroma of seasoned onions and potatoes sweeps his way. Quietly, he opens wide the door and lets in the light, and halting underneath the lintel, surveys the room. Aside from the girl it is empty; he expected to see at least two people. His attention is arrested by a wooden rocking horse that stands in front of the window by the entrance. It is an exquisite specimen with bold eyes, a tiny head and short back from which sprouts a magnificent tail set high. He assesses its well-proportioned beauty with the judgment of someone who knows what to look for; but the underlying memory attached to this one does not surface.

He hears a sharp intake of breath followed by a loud clatter, and startled, turns to his right; the metal lid of a vessel is spinning on its axis and the young woman is backing away, her eyes wide with fright. She brings up her hands to cover her face and an elbow knocks down a candle from its shelf.

"*Ghabroo nako*," he says, stepping back, the jangle of metal against stone sending spasms through his body. She lowers her hands and crosses them in front of her neck. "*Ghabroo nako*."

"Who are you?" she says, snatching up a rolling pin, this time knocking a salt shaker to the ground. Ignoring the spill, she moves forward until she is halfway between him and the metal hob, the wooden cylinder thrust out in front of her as though it were a fencing sword.

His tongue is pushing thickly against the ceiling of his mouth; he unpeels it and says this time in English, "I frightened you." His tone is apologetic.

She lowers the pin, her expression suddenly calm. "Ah!" she says. "You must be the stray Pappy brought home last night. Your door was closed when I left this morning. I didn't expect you'd still be here."

Her voice has a pleasing lilt.

"I'm not going to use this, you must know," she says, lifting the pin, "unless you come near me." She points towards the armchair next to the rocking horse. "Sit down there and if you are very still, I will give you a bowl of soup. I have the ears of an elephant is what Pappy says, and if you move a muscle I shall know, even though my back is turned." She returns to the hob and he takes a seat, against the window.

The young woman stirs the pot gently, over and over again, as though whatever she is cooking might stick to the bottom.

He settles further into his chair and looks around. A spiral staircase leads to an upper floor and a cot with a bookcase next to it stands opposite the piano. His gaze keeps returning to the checkered blanket saddling the rocking horse, but he is too shy to reach over and use it to cover his frozen toes. The young woman is humming, replicating with sweetness the tune she earlier played on the piano, and as he closes his eyes she begins to sing in a language he cannot understand.

The next thing he knows, her slippered foot is nudging him awake. "Time to eat." She points towards the table and a bowl from which steam is rising.

"I'd like to use the lavatory," he says, and is immediately pleased by the cohesiveness of his sentence.

She grabs a hurricane lamp and after lighting it, thrusts it into his hand. "You'd best wear your shoes." He notices for the first time that her narrow eyes are wide set and that her upper lip possesses an odd shadowed dip.

Daylight is waning as he makes his way to the farther end of the yard. When he is done, he lingers in the fragrant garden, tracking with his eyes the drifting moon. The sky is porous and soft, speckled with loosely spun clouds. At his feet flowers nod in raised beds and a scent of fecundity fills the air. Shivering, he examines his surroundings until he can no longer ignore his stomach's lusty growls. The cottage windows are illuminated golden; he hurries in.

The woman protests that he took so long to return that now his food has turned cold. She grabs his bowl off the table and overturns its cooling contents into the bubbling pot.

Contrite, he reaches for the enamel water jug standing inside a basin on the scratched cabinet, drying his hands afterwards on a napkin bordered by lace. He eats at the table next to the piano, glancing every so often at the young woman, who is looking intently out the window, the lower half of her body twitching now and again.

She says, "Pappy is at The Wild Pheasant tonight. It's Thursday and that is why he is late. I should walk down the hill to fetch him, but he knows his way."

Puzzled by her words, the man thinks that along with his memory he has lost his ability to interpret speech. He has yet to fathom whom she was speaking to while playing the piano. He says, "Mr. Owens is your father?"

"Yes."

"And your mother—"

"Underground and in a grave so far away that I must cross several oceans to see it." Her snorted giggle contradicts the sedateness of her eyes.

Reddening, he looks down into his bowl.

"There's no need to be embarrassed," she says. "It's over two decades, you must know, since she left this world." She continues to watch him eat.

Uncomfortable, he shifts in his chair and turns his face away slightly, so as not to appear rude.

Continuing to scrutinize him, she says, "I ought to introduce myself. My name is Catherine. What's yours?"

"I don't know," he says without looking up.

"You don't know?" Before she can continue to express her incredulity, they hear the sound of a footfall and the unlatching of a gate. "Here's Pappy!" she says, opening the door. As soon as Mr. Owens presents himself, she looks at her father in a questioning manner, her face tilted towards the stranger at the table. The man quickly soaks the last of his soup with the heel of his bread, and when he raises his head, there is a rueful expression on his face.

"No wiser to your identity than when I left you this morning, I see," Mr. Owens responds, handing Catherine his cap. He stands by the cold fireplace and addresses his guest, enunciating for emphasis: "*Kay-say-ho?*"

The seated man is baffled and does not know how to respond.

Mr. Owens looks at his daughter, who is standing against the metal hob, an equally mystified expression on her face. "Hundreds of languages where this lad comes from and I know odd sentences from merely one." He scratches his head.

"But he speaks English, Pappy," Catherine says. Suddenly her face brightens. "He's Indian then?" There is curiosity in her tone, and wonder, as though the stranger is a specimen she has heard much about and long waited to see.

Her father nods. "Yes, as far as I can tell."

Relieved and suddenly hopeful, the lost man dabs his mouth with a handkerchief. Instinct tells him that Mr. Owens is to be trusted and that if he thinks his guest is Indian—even though the word has no familiar ring to it—then he will take it to be true. Leaning forward and pushing away his empty soup bowl, he awaits further revelations from his host.

Mr. Owens says, "My daughter and I, we were both born in India. Catherine was a mere child when I brought her here. She remembers nothing about her birthplace. Nevertheless, her fascination for it continues." So saying, he lifts the hurricane lamp and walks out into the darkness.

Disappointment causing his forehead to break into a sweat, the man pushes back in his chair and stares at the blank wall in front of him, thinking that his host's connection to India is likely what prompted him to offer a perfect stranger refuge inside his home.

When Mr. Owens returns, he says to his daughter who is scrubbing a pot at the basin, "Everything all right?"

Ignoring his question, she asks, "When are you going to tell me the full story about what happened at the pub last night?"

The man remembers the narrow, stone-flagged room with long wooden tables and benches, the foreign-tongued locals crowding around him, urging him to examine the contents of his pockets: a soggy handkerchief and a buttoned leather wallet thick with notes and coins. It is everything that happened before The Wild Pheasant that has been erased from his memory.

Mr. Owens takes a chair opposite the guest at the table. Catherine finishes drying the pot and sits next to him.

"When I went to the pub after supper last evening," Mr. Owens tells her, "our lad was sitting all hunched up in one corner at the end of a bench. His teeth were chattering, and his eyes were half-closed with fatigue. Bob and Jones had found him earlier, wandering lost and dishevelled this side of Plas Coch. He was hungry, and parched as a drought-stricken field. I asked Stan to get him something to eat. When he was done eating, I brought him here. Jones cautioned me against taking in a stranger but I have a sixth sense about such things. Besides, if I'd left you there," Mr. Owens addresses the man, "how would you have fended for yourself? Where would you have gone? You'd been at the pub since late afternoon and hadn't thought to ask for water, leave alone food." He leans forward in his chair. "Tore into that stew you did, along with a mound of carrots and potatoes. Just as well you are up here and not in London, where the rations are barely enough to keep even small children from starving."

The man is once again perplexed.

Mr. Owens appears not to notice as he struggles out of his coat and hangs it from the back of his chair. "How's the head?" he asks.

The man grimaces as his fingers reach up and probe the swelling.

His benefactor gets up from the table and placing a gentle hand on the man's neck, tips forward his head so he can examine the wound. "See that nasty bump, Catherine? The blow must have knocked the wind out of him, along with his memory."

"Shouldn't he see Dr. Cotter?"

"He was at the pub last evening. Said the lad's amnesia reminded him of a case he had come across in the last war." Mr. Owens addresses the man. "You do remember what Dr. Cotter told you? That you will one day regain your memory?"

The man nods, shivering. A brisk breeze is blowing in through the window.

Mr. Owens asks Catherine to fetch a thick pair of socks and the largest cardigan she can find.

"But it's a warm evening," she says.

"Believe me, my Cat, when I say that their coldest day is far hotter than our warmest."

Watching his guest slip on the borrowed socks, Mr. Owens asks what he would like to be called until such time as he can remember his name. The man shrugs.

"Let's call him Hari. From that story, *Hari, the conjuror*," Catherine says.

"Shall we call you Hari then?"

The man gives a nod of assent.

Mr. Owens turns to his daughter, who is now laying the table. "You all right, Catherine?"

"You already asked me," she says, glancing swiftly at the young man who now has an alias.

Hari moves to the armchair next to the rocking horse as father and daughter sit down to supper.

"Eat quickly, pet," Mr. Owens urges, pushing towards Catherine a glass of water to which he has added half a teaspoon of what looks like powdered sugar. "And drink up before you go to bed. There's been too much excitement tonight."

After Mr. Owens is done eating, he applies some ointment to the back of Hari's head then hands him another fever cordial. And as the man returns to his room, he drills himself over and over again: "*Tuze nau Hari ahey*. Your name is Hari."

He changes quickly, and sliding underneath the blankets, brings them up to cover his throbbing head. The cordial produces hallucinations. At the end of a fitful sleep he awakens with a constricted throat and a taste of salt on his tongue, the remnant of the sea he has been dreaming about all night, of water forcing its way into the cabin as he and the peculiar Catherine try to stay afloat, desperate to escape its rising tide. To the frantic tattoo of a branch tapping against the windowpane, he snuggles once again underneath the stiff blankets, and pushing his fingers deep into his temples tries to dislodge whatever is blocking his recollection. When nothing stirs, he turns on his side and lets the despondency that has been accumulating run down and wet his pillow.

~ TWO ~

THE SPRINGS SQUEAK AS Hari sits up in bed. The wound at the back of his head is less sore and the ache inside it almost gone. All of a sudden remembering the doctor's encouraging prognosis, he enters the kitchen with renewed hope. His host is standing over a large vessel filled with steaming water. The door leading into the backyard is open. Catherine is nowhere to be seen.

Mr. Owens greets him, adding, "I've left a clean set of clothes, my own, on that chair, if you wish to change into something fresh."

"Thank you," Hari says, gratified once again by the old man's thoughtful generosity. "Where can I bathe?"

Mr. Owens points to what appears to be a cupboard underneath the staircase.

Hari opens the door and drapes his borrowed clothes and towel on a brass hook. He returns to the kitchen and brings back with him the large, heated vessel that his host, in spite of Hari's protests, helps him carry. They pour the hot water into the galvanized tub.

Shrugging out of his pyjamas, Hari looks out the window; to the left is a sloping hill, a spreading ash tree leans to the right. A pegged clothesline from which are fluttering washed clothes stands alongside a wooden trough. The grass on the knoll is rippling in the breeze and a blackbird with orange beak watches the world with beady eye. Hari steps into the tub and douses himself with its fast-cooling water, running his tongue over gritty teeth. Intimidated anew by the challenges facing him, the same questions circle his head: Who am I? How did I end up here? Where shall I go next?

The brown trousers and checked shirt he slips into are not overly tight though much too short at sleeve and trouser leg. After rinsing his soiled clothes underneath the cold-water tap, he hangs them outside on the clothesline to dry. Re-entering the cottage, he stands in front of the cabinet mirror and examines his features in the hope that its details will yield some clues; all he sees are bloodshot eyes and over-grown hair and a face that is so pale and pinched that he almost does not recognize it.

His host walks down the spiral staircase. After inform-ing Hari that Catherine has left for work, Mr. Owens asks him to take a seat at the table. Over tea and toast he says, "Now that you've had a good night's sleep, let's see if we can unravel some of your past." Mr. Owens' smile is touched by empathy. "First, let us consider what we know. One. . ." he holds up a forefinger, "found by two men this side of Plas Coch a short distance from Snowdon."

"Snowdon?"

"The highest mountain in Wales."

Hari's face remains blank.

"You perhaps remember London, the capital city of Great Britain?"

When Hari does not respond, Mr. Owens pulls out an atlas and opens it to the appropriate page. "We are here in North Wales. And here is London. Mount Snowdon as you can see is to the north and west of it."

Mr. Owens opens the book to the map of India and leaves the table to make more tea. When nothing looks familiar, Hari shuts the atlas and picks up his toast.

"What else do we know?" Mr. Owens says, returning to the table with a fresh cup. "You come from India, as evidenced by the holy thread that runs diagonally across your chest—I noticed it when you were undressing Wednesday night before slipping into my pyjamas. Your accent, the clear, stressed manner in which you pronounce our English words, is familiar to me. And even though the colour of your skin is olive, not brown, I have seen enough pale-skinned, grey-eyed Indians to recognize that you come in all shades and sizes. And yes, by the way you brought your hands together in front of your chest when you thanked me." The old man holds up a third finger. "What else do we know?"

"Can we make a list of all the things we don't know?"

"That might take several days, don't you think?" Mr. Owens raises one eyebrow, his expression comical.

In spite of his plunging mood, Hari smiles.

"Do you know what year it is?" His host's tone is doubtful.

Hari grimaces; he has no idea.

"It is 1942, and a very sad 1942 for there has been a ferocious war going on for almost three years now, and it's spread to nearly every part of the world. We, the Allied forces, are not winning it, but one day we will, of that I am certain."

Hari tries to elicit a suitable response even as Mr. Owens expounds on Hitler's Germany and the Axis powers, explains the position of Great Britain and her allies, and enumerates the battles that have been won and lost, but all he can feel is a chilly disengagement.

"You don't look like a soldier to me," the old man says. "Used more to luxury than hardship, I would say."

Almost by instinct, Hari concurs.

"A tourist? A student? Unlikely. It is only a misguided man who would choose to venture abroad in such uncertain times."

Hari stops fidgeting in his chair and listens with concentration, ready to place his thumb on any lever that will spring open the door of his sealed memories.

His host's voice drops to a whisper, "You could be a spy."

Hari gives Mr. Owens a skeptical look.

They both laugh.

"That's more like it," Mr. Owens says. "A little humour can go a long way." He asks Hari to follow him outside.

They climb a flight of open stairs that lead to the attic. At the farthest end of the unpartitioned room sits a large trunk. With the wind whistling through the cracked walls, an unseen weather vane creaking on rusty hinges, Mr. Owens removes one by one the scant contents of the dusty, battered chest. There are stained silk cushions, a clumped bunch of peacock feathers, a tall brass hookah, and a thin rug on which is imprinted the face of a tiger, its mouth open in a snarl.

"Anything look familiar?" Mr. Owens asks.

Hari shakes his head. Nothing is stranger to him than the contents of this trunk, its objects as alien and dilapidated as the condition of this house.

While replacing the shabby items, Mr. Owens suggests that Hari make his way to London. Perhaps he registered at India House upon his arrival, whenever that might have been.

Hari is immediately agreeable to this idea; an urgent desire to leave this place has been claiming his thoughts ever since he opened his eyes in the morning. As they walk down the stairs, Mr. Owens proposes they visit the post office to find out the departure time for the bus to Llandudno Junction, from where Hari will catch a train to Chester and then another to London. Back in the sitting room, Mr. Owens removes a raincoat and cap from a box underneath the cot and hands them to his guest. Hari shrugs into the coat. It is three-quarter length and lined with cottonwool, and he is immediately grateful for its warmth.

Birdsong fills the air as the two men walk down the hill. A stone wall covered in moss borders the pastureland to their right, a farmhouse nestled in dense wood lies in the valley to their left. Birds fly in and out of overhanging trees, displacing branches that shower on Hari cold, frosty water. Mr. Owens is relating the history of Wales, but Hari registers little. Afterwards, he will remember a small part of his host's monologue: that Wales was conquered by the Romans roughly two thousand years ago; that the conquerors left a legacy of advanced agricultural practices and most likely introduced sheep to the countryside.

Twenty minutes later they are in the village square. The man inside the post office is helpful and tells Hari that the next bus to Llandudno Junction will leave at three o' clock next Friday afternoon, the fourteenth of August.

"Nothing earlier?" Mr. Owens asks.

"Normally there would be, but on account of petrol rationing, direct service to large towns has been reduced."

Hari turns to Mr. Owens in dismay.

"You can continue to stay with us," his host kindly says.

Thinking he would much rather walk to Llandudno Junction, Hari nonetheless manages to muster a thankful smile. They climb back up the hill, and to dispel the disappointment that inhabits his heart, Hari reminds himself that he will be required to stay in this village for only a week, and in order to urge time along, he will spend a large portion of his hours reading the newspapers he has bought at the corner shop in the hope that something in their content will stimulate his memory. But as soon as the placid cottage comes into view, panic once again grips him.

It is late afternoon before Catherine returns home. Hari informs her that Mr. Owens said he would be back at six o' clock and that she should start preparing supper without waiting for him. She slumps into a dining chair without acknowledging Hari's message. His heart already weighed down by everything he has read in the news, none of which has been recognizable, Hari feels further discomfited by her silence. He goes back to his newspaper and pretends to read even as he watches Catherine, who is holding her head between her hands, pressing her palms every now and then against her ears. She tosses her head and brings forward her plait and all of a sudden there comes to him a fleeting image of a girl unravelling her braided hair while seated in front of a mirror. Buoyed, he closes his eyes and wills his mind to go back to that forgotten place, but unhappily there is only the imprint of Catherine huddled over the table, framed by a dark window. The silence draws a tighter net around him. Hari would like to breach it, but something in her demeanour is forbidding. Glancing repeatedly at the front door, she pushes back her chair and runs up the stairs to her room.

When Mr. Owens returns, Hari describes Catherine's behaviour and says he's afraid that she might not be well. In response, his host removes an almost empty bottle from the glass-fronted cupboard next to the rocking horse and shakes onto his palm a few tiny pills. He carries them with a glass of water up to Catherine, returning downstairs a few minutes later.

After Mr. Owens has finished preparing supper, he calls out to her. She walks haltingly down the stairs, her eyes heavy-lidded and unfocused, and takes her place at the table. Mr. Owens tells Hari that Catherine's cousin Eileen runs a day nursery, and that ever since the young woman previously employed by her left the village to join the war, Catherine has been giving Eileen a much-needed hand. He smiles, clearly proud of his daughter.

They eat in silence and afterwards, before the table is cleared and the crumbs wiped away, and although it is yet too early for bedtime, Mr. Owens urges Catherine to retire for it has been another long day.

When Hari enters the kitchen in the middle of the night for a glass of water, he hears her humming upstairs. He leaves the half-drunk glass by the basin, returns to bed and covers his ears to blot out the mournful tune.

A shaded road runs from the base of the Snowdonia mountains into the village of Betws-y-Coed, winding through untamed countryside that is a dazzling collage of high moorland and dramatic ravines, crisscrossed by rivers that tumble and water the fertile pastures before emptying themselves westwards into the sea. Mr. Owens' cottage lies somewhere off this road, encircled by wooded hills. His host informs Hari of all of this as they sit in a scrap of sunlight the following Monday afternoon, watching young football players in the village green. Every now and then Hari shyly cheers on the underdogs, sturdy young boys who have on their team one or two weak players who get pushed and out-muscled from time to time.

Mr. Owens looks at Hari in surprise. "You know football, do you? Maybe played some yourself?"

"Perhaps." The team camaraderie causes inside of Hari a veiled surge of recognition.

His host looks across the green and waves. "Pete's

lending me his van today. I have to make a delivery ten miles up the road. Do you wish to stay here or come with me?"

Hari gets to his feet, not at all wanting to be left behind.

Pete, whose sprinkle of grey hair forms a patchy cap above his red ears, hands Mr. Owens the ignition key. They drive away in the battered van, its inside odour evoking sheep manure and damp wool. The narrow lanes are winding and the pavement is slippery, covered here and there with wet, flattened leaves. After making a sharp turn, Mr. Owens steers his way to a solitary stone house that overlooks a sloping field. The sky is littered with hastening clouds and in the distance hungry sheep are trimming grass. The two men walk up a muddy path to the front door. Mr. Owens unlocks it and ushers Hari inside. In the centre of a workroom stands a reddish-brown miniature wooden horse of aristocratic bearing, its expression meek and placid, its eyes gentle and deep. The fittings of saddle, reins and rocker are painted bright yellow, red and green.

Hari sees himself doubled over a steed, galloping neck to neck with another; the gilded image disappears all too swiftly. Mr. Owens is saying, "A pure Welsh pony, this little fellow is."

Hari runs his hand over the smooth, painted wood. A pile of half-prepared timber releases into the air a refreshing smell of wood scrapings and sap. And all at once it occurs to him that Mr. Owens is a skilled carpenter, an accomplished woodcarver, and the craftsman of the rocking horse in the cottage. Hari helps haul the wooden horse onto the back of the van, and after the pony is covered in sacks and secured with rope, Mr. Owens steers away the vehicle at a slow, steady pace.

As they drive away, the old man tries to teach Hari Welsh. Hari stumbles over the pronunciations. "The Welsh tongue is the very devil to learn," Mr. Owens asserts. "I don't know that I would have picked it up after moving here if my father had not insisted I learn it right from the day I was born. My mother was English. She met my father when he was posted in Calcutta on army duty. After they were married, they settled in Patna." Mr. Owens leans forward and peers at the raindrops that are beginning to plummet. "The cottage and the land where I carve the horses belonged to my Welsh grandparents. My father was their only child. I inherited the property after he died."

"That's when you came here."

Mr. Owens nods. "It wasn't an easy decision to make. Catherine was very young and I'd visited my grandparents but twice. A small financial settlement that was a part of the bequest enabled our move. Sometimes I wish we'd remained in India."

Mr. Owens is quiet the rest of the way, and not until the horse is delivered and the money pocketed and the deftness of his hands praised by the satisfied new owners does he regain his humour. Aided by a clearing sky, the summer evening turns tolerable. They return the van to Pete, who is waiting for them at The Wild Pheasant. Mr. Owens has a quick pint before they make their way back to the cottage. The slowly setting sun is so warm that Hari undoes the top two buttons of his shirt.

The gate creaks loudly as Mr. Owens pushes against it, but Catherine, who is facing them on the garden bench, does not look up. She is leaning over, staring intently at the ground as though in a trance, her arms dangling between her knees. Mr. Owens puts out his hand to stop Hari from going forward and silently points him towards the back of the cottage.

The door leading into the kitchen is unlatched. Gripped by an acute sense of disquiet, Hari plucks a random book from a squat cupboard, and as he is straightening up a dizzy spell overtakes him. Seated in the armchair, his back turned to the window so as not to see what is happening with Catherine and Mr. Owens, he looks down at the book he is holding. It is the first of an eight-volume set and has a reddish leather binding on which is written in gold and Latinate lettering the title: *Middlemarch*. On the spine is the name of the author: George Eliot. Hari opens the pages to Chapter I and without much effort is soon absorbed in the affairs of an upper-class English family, the Brookes of Tipton.

The room is beginning to turn dark when he hears running footsteps. The front door swings open and Catherine stands in the doorway, her fierce-looking eyes pinpoints of concentration. Mr. Owens is close on her heels. "Don't let her get away," he says.

Hari flings down the book and standing at the bottom of the staircase, blocks the way to the kitchen door. Without losing a moment, Catherine turns around, and cupping her right palm over her left upper arm, hurls herself at her father. Mr. Owens stumbles sideways under Catherine's weight and the key with which he has locked the front door drops to the ground.

Hari moves forward and pockets it. He pries Catherine away from her father, pins her bony shoulder blades against his chest, then wraps one arm around her waist. Mr. Owens is now at the wall-mounted cupboard next to the piano, plucking from it a tiny packet. He instructs Catherine to open her mouth before emptying the packet's powdery contents down her throat. He fills a glass of water and places it against her lips. She takes great noisy gulps, and Hari is about to release her when Mr. Owens says, "Don't let her go."

The minutes pass and it seems to Hari that he has been standing there forever; the back of his knees are aching, his head is jangling, and the sweat beading his forehead betrays the effort of holding Catherine's strength against his own. At last Mr. Owens motions to the cot opposite the piano.

Catherine cannot walk and Hari is forced to carry her. He sets her down and she curls away instantly, closing her eyes. Her father examines her left arm. It is only then that Hari notices the two deep punctures from which thin streams of blood are running into her palm. He keeps his gaze averted even as Mr. Owens cleans and bathes the wounds, and binds them with a strip of cloth. Afterwards, he doffs his cap in Hari's direction, and tells him that his presence of mind saved the day.

Embarrassed, Hari brushes off the suggestion.

But Mr. Owens insists. "I wouldn't have known where to begin to look for her in the woods had she escaped," he says.

He walks to the rocking horse and slides to the ground and sits there cross-legged, his back unsupported and erect. "My prior association with India," he says, "has taught me two things: how to eat spicy food with relish and how to sit on the floor. Both aid digestion, I believe." He lights his pipe, and slowly the vigour returns to his face.

Hari retrieves his book from the floor but is unable to concentrate.

"What happened?" he asks at last, hoping that there is a benign explanation for how Catherine came by her wounds.

Mr. Owens does not offer a direct reply. "I'm at the end of my rope," he says, "even though I can ill afford to be. Old school friends, the last of whom she is losing by the minute, my pathetic guidance, an inherited disease; how much longer will I be able to battle such odds?"

Hari does not know what to say.

The old man gets to his feet and drags his armchair closer to the cot. Catherine is asleep now and breathing deeply.

"They institutionalized my mother when I was so young that I hardly remember her face," Mr. Owens continues. "Even though I do remember the sanatorium where she lived. That's how Father used to refer to it, although the servants, and even our friends when he was out of earshot, called it the madhouse. It was situated in a hill station up in Assam and had a long roof on which monkeys played. The sly creatures had upright tails and eager eyes and it seemed to me that they knew all my secrets: that I wet my bed, that I stammered, that I walked in my sleep. They frightened me. The curious thing is that I don't recollect ever meeting Mother. Just the monkeys on the rooftops, and the gagging smell of urine mingled with disinfectant."

Hari is acutely discomfited by the intimacy of these recollections. But, his host is in a mood to reminisce and the least Hari can do is listen.

"Much else about my childhood is forgotten. Perhaps I choose not to remember it. But I'll never forget the day Memi, my Ayah, told me to wash up because Father was waiting for me at the Gymkhana. She accompanied me there, and when in spite of repeated messages he did not come out, she deposited me in a chair outside its pavilion. I waited, watching with envy the ball boys play a game of marbles outside the tennis courts." Mr. Owens relights his pipe. "When Father finally appeared, smelling of drink, everyone but the watchman had gone home. It was the first time it occurred to me that I hated Father—for the pathetic condition of his breath and dress, his frosty neglect of me, and above all for keeping Mother so far away, in Assam. Memi was waiting up for us when we returned to our cottage and it was she who told me about the passing away of Mother when I awoke the following morning. I was seven years old."

The old man has led a cursed life, Hari thinks, his heart clutched by unnamed dread. He transfers *Middlemarch* back to its shelf and retreats to his room. All is dark outside the window, only the far-flung sky holding distant points of light. A star is plummeting into the vastness when Mr. Owens comes in and hands him a bowl.

"Eat quickly now, before the food turns cold."

"Where's your supper?"

"We'll have it together afterwards, the sleeping beauty and I." In spite of the attempt at humour, Mr. Owens' voice cracks.

Hari eats, the contents of his bowl tasting like broken bits of bread over which hot water has been poured and salt and pepper added. It is mushy and palatable only because he is so hungry.

"My biggest fear," Mr. Owens says, sitting on the chair in Hari's room, "is that they will institutionalize my Cat. I won't allow it, of course."

"Who will?"

"The doctors. Today you were here and could stop her from hurting herself." The old man starts to say something then shuts his mouth; his expression is bleak.

Later, when Hari is stretched out on his cot, Mr. Owens calls out that Catherine will not awaken, not for a long time, and that if Hari wishes, he is most welcome to accompany him to The Wild Pheasant. Hari declines. After Mr. Owens' footsteps have died away, he steps out of his room. Averting his eyes from Catherine on the cot, he removes a coat from its peg and steps outside. The garden is enveloped by darkness but loathe to return indoors, he stumbles his way around its periphery. After a final glance at the moon banked by a ring of clouds, he walks back inside the cottage. Sagging into the armchair and with one leg outstretched, he kicks the rocking horse into continuous motion, and keeps kicking until the steed is in full gallop, hinges squeaking.

~ THREE ~

WHEN HARI AWAKENS THE next morning and right away probes the wound on the back of his head, he is astonished to find that it is almost healed.

In the sitting room, Catherine is no longer on her cot. Through the kitchen door he can see his host in the back garden, raking dead leaves away from a planted vegetable bed. He lights a flame beneath the water-filled vessel and after rinsing his mouth at the basin, dons his sweater and joins Mr. Owens outside. The rolling hills are covered in a fine mist and some unseen hand is chopping kindling, the sharp, ring-ing echo of axe against wood bouncing off the shed.

"How's Catherine?" he asks.

"Better. She's resting upstairs."

They return to the kitchen and sit at the table and drink tea. Hari reaches forward and picks up a square inch of sharply-creased newsprint that is lying next to the sugar caddy. It holds traces of the powder Mr. Owens had poured into Catherine's mouth the previous evening.

"That medicine was sent to me from India," Mr. Owens says. "Back in those days, the driver of my dear friend Harold would get these fits. I happened to witness an episode one day. Just like that, the man began to writhe and foam at the mouth and before he could swallow his tongue, Harold pinched his nose and forced some powder down his throat; it calmed him immediately. I never forgot that incident and when the trouble with Catherine started, and Dr. Cotter said he couldn't do anything for her, I wrote Harold and requested that he obtain a powder suited to her needs. He knows Mother's history and obliged me right away. Every time my stock dwindles, he sends me more."

"How long has Catherine been ill?"

"A good four years, ever since she turned twenty-one."

"Do the powders work?"

"Yes, they do. But, how much longer will I be able to administer them without supervision? And what if by tranquilizing her, I am in effect doing harm?"

Hari can tell Mr. Owens has asked himself these questions many times before and is weary for lack of answers.

"You go on now and have your bath," he tells Hari, "No

need to entangle yourself in our affairs. Here today, gone tomorrow, and that's the way it must be." In spite of this assertion, Mr. Owens' tone is regretful. In the bathroom, Hari makes a vow that on Friday he will wait at the bus stop a full two hours ahead of its scheduled departure time, just to be sure of catching it.

Later that morning, Hari is reading *Middlemarch* when Mr. Owen asks if he would like to accompany him down to the village. They walk to the butcher and the old man produces his ration card and is given what is due him and some more because everyone knows he has a guest he is obliged to feed. At the grocers' they buy a few onions, some potatoes, a small head of cabbage, and carrots that are orange and stout. Mr. Owens points to some domestic goods on the shelf. Hari selects a toothbrush, the last of the toothpaste, soap and a shaving kit. On the windowsill are cupcakes covered in white icing topped by a sprinkling of minute silver balls. Hari asks for half a dozen. Earlier, at the butcher's, he offered to pay but Mr. Owens said that there was no need to settle up right away, that he would square his bill like always at the end of the month. So now Hari makes a sign to the grocer to add the meagre vegetables to his own purchases. The man is complicit. Armed with their packages, they return to the cottage under a brightening sun.

Catherine is leaning against the stove, staring at her reflection in the back of a ladle. Mr. Owens waves his hand in greeting. His daughter puts down the scoop and retreats into a corner, eyes fixed on her father, pupils dull. Hari is moved by the contrast with the lively girl who brandished a rolling pin at him mere days ago. Mr. Owens toasts bread on a toasting fork. He butters it and lays it in the windowsill next to Catherine. She eats hungrily as Hari watches from the armchair.

"Do you remember what happened yesterday, pet?" Mr. Owens gently asks.

Catherine reaches up and strokes her upper arm still bound in cloth. Her expression is sullen.

"It's those voices. They told you to do that, didn't they?" There is unbridled frustration in Mr. Owens' tone even as he says, "Difficult as it is for you to ignore them, you must not give in, Catherine! Fight the bloody buggers, why can't you?"

Catherine is silent.

Hari places two cupcakes on a plate on the kitchen table and looking at Catherine murmurs that she should try them. When she does not respond, he tells Mr. Owens that he will go for a walk.

Opening the side gate, he stubs his foot on a jagged stone. Catherine is not the only one hearing voices. He is hearing them too and his voices are saying: *leave, leave, leave, now, now, now* . . . He sets off down the hill, plodding through muddy pasture, keeping a cautionary eye on two bulls that are snorting and bellowing only a short distance away. The sun massages his back and as the cottage disappears behind a rise he hears the sound of crashing water. He cannot see its source on account of the woods that tower before him, thick and solid like a wall. In a sudden burst of energy he runs towards the trees, betting against himself that if he can make his way to the river and drink from it within the next ten minutes, it will be a sure sign that he will have recovered his memory before the end of day.

He reaches the edge of the wood, and stumbles through the undergrowth. The roar of the water is deafening now. Through the trees he sees a steel grey ribbon, and his mind's eye flashes to a narrow canal where water flows along placidly. Hari stops in his tracks, but when no other memories surface, he approaches the river and leans forward to search for a suitable place to kneel, and as he does so, loses his balance and finds himself up to his waist in cold churning water. Clutching an overhanging branch, he heaves himself up out of the current, and hurls his weight onto the bank.

His heart beating rapidly, he lies supine for a minute. When he raises himself on his elbows, he knows he is lost. He stands and starts walking in the direction in which he thinks the cottage lies. It is more than an hour before he can see the top of Mr. Owens' chimney breathing out a dying thread of smoke. He climbs the hill, his head hammering with pain, his limbs stiff, his body wet and chilled to the bone. In the yard he sheds his clothes and leaves them in a heap to be washed later on. He removes from the clothes-line Mr. Owens' borrowed garments, steps into them, and enters the cottage on tiptoe in case Catherine is resting. There is a note from Mr. Owens saying that they have gone to cousin Eileen's, for tea. The P.S. reads: *Bread and cheese are on the table.*

The opaque silence of the narrow house deepening his loneliness, Hari carries his food to the front door and eats underneath its lintel. The sky is a soft blue and sunshine teeming with golden specks is slanting in through the trees. After he has returned his empty plate to the kitchen, he takes two blankets and a pillow from his bed and set-tles on the bench alongside the house's outer wall. Covering himself in coarse wool, the occasional wasp buzzing around his head and chattering birds casting moving shadows on the birdbath, he falls into deep slumber made feverish by startling dreams. When he awakens, the garden is silent and the sinking sun is hovering just above the hills. He returns inside, skin rippled with goose bumps, and makes tea.

As darkness falls, he reads to the end of Chapter 5 of *Middlemarch*, struggling to concentrate, drinking hot water to warm his insides, occasionally wondering when Mr. Owens and Catherine will return. When it is entirely dark, he lights the coal fire. An agitated feeling sours his stomach. Stretching his legs towards the flames, he raises his voice and informs the walls, floors and ceiling: *Only a few days and I will be gone; only a few.*

The following morning Mr. Owens is standing by his bed. "You look flushed," the old man says. "I need to check your forehead."

Hari remembers stumbling from the armchair to his room, his feet deadened by the cold. Now he flinches from his host's cold touch and blinks at the bright light shining through the open window. He can hear Catherine playing the piano and everything feels familiar, as though he has lived it many times before.

"Fever!" Mr. Owens proclaims. "That's what you get for walking along the edge of the river. I saw your shoes, soaking wet they were, and the heap of muddied clothes. Received a proper dunking, I reckon. You are making quite a habit, I'd say, of falling ill on my watch."

Hari feels genuine remorse.

Mr. Owens' expression brightens as he glances over his shoulder. "Playing the piano is always a good sign. And by the look of things, the next time Catherine's health takes another turn, you just may be here to lend me a hand."

His host's unlucky words prickling inside his head, Hari says, "I'm determined to catch that bus on Friday, you must know."

Mr. Owens looks at him skeptically but does not speak his mind. Instead he says, "It is imperative that you find out who you are. The whole village is hoping for it. The war has been going on much too long and enough families have been separated, some forever."

Once again, the mention of war increases Hari's feeling of alienation.

Mr. Owens pulls forward a chair. "Some men who were at The Wild Pheasant that first night combed the place where you were found. They wanted to see if they could locate any of your belongings."

"And?"

"They found nothing."

Before he can give a thought to what he is saying, Hari finds himself blurting out, "Won't you come with me to London?"

A look of pleasant surprise crosses Mr. Owens' face. "I cannot leave Catherine," he says. "But you will be fine on your own and when you have regained your memory, don't forget to come back and tell us about it."

~

For supper Catherine serves sausages, marmalade and boiled peas. Her movements are deft and purposeful; her expression is alert. Halfway through the meal, Hari lays down his cutlery. The sausage untouched on his plate, he excuses himself, saying he is feeling too ill to eat. He just barely makes it to his bed, and burrowing under the blankets soon falls asleep. When he opens his eyes, a crescent moon is rising, and his throat feels scratchy and raw. On his right shin there is a burning sensation. He stumbles to the lavatory underneath a fine drizzle and, after carrying the water jug out to the garden, he rinses his hands in bushes that are dripping with rain. Seized with thirst, he throws back his head and catches the droplets in his mouth.

The kitchen is deserted. Hari drains the fever cordial that Mr. Owens has left out for him and ignores the slice of bread beside it. He crawls back into bed and within no time is sweating, his swollen shin throbbing at the slightest movement. He sits up and traces with a gentle, circular motion its edge and then moving his fingers inwards he delicately probes the deep gash at its centre; pain shoots up his leg.

Unable to get out of bed the following day, Hari is grateful when Mr. Owens heaps upon him extra blankets and once again feeds him warm cordials. By evening he is able to hobble to the fireplace. Catherine is also under the weather, and is resting upstairs. Hari feels more aware than ever that Catherine requires a lot of attention and that in spite of his warm hospitality, Mr. Owens could not have given shelter to a stranger at a worse time. But for Hari right now, there is a graver concern.

"You won't be able to catch that Friday bus," Mr. Owens declares, echoing Hari's thoughts.

Hari is put out by his host's cheerful assertion; he'd much rather his commiseration. "Bloody hell!" he says.

"Go on, then. Let loose and curse. Don't be such a gentleman, Hari. Lift up that fist to heaven. Bloody hell, indeed!"

Mr. Owens passes Hari a mug of beef tea, so hot that Hari drinks it in small mincing gulps. His host cuts himself a slice of bread and says Hari must not have any because it is better to starve a fever than to feed it.

The home remedies don't work, and Hari feels no better. He is forced to admit that it would be madness to try and leave the village in this state.

On Friday morning, Mr. Owens insists that Hari visit Dr. Cotter, whose office is in a two-storey stone house at the bottom of a steep road; wind-whipped flowerbeds line the path to its entrance. The doctor is standing in the entrance of his surgery, smoking a cigarette. He is wide of girth and thick of wrist. "Not Catherine again?" he addresses Mr. Owens. "I told you, Denbigh Asylum is where you need to take her."

Mr. Owens looks pained but collects himself. "It's the Indian boy," he says.

"Not recovered his memory, I take it."

Hari grimaces. The doctor's tone is much too careless, as though Hari's loss is of little consequence.

Inside the surgery, Hari suppresses a groan even as he hauls himself up onto the examining table.

"Have you been eating?" Dr. Cotter asks.

"Only some broth," Hari says.

The doctor places the back of his fingers against Hari's neck. "You shouldn't have brought him here, Owens. The man is burning up. I would have made a house call."

As if on cue, Hari's teeth begin to chatter. Dr. Cotter pulls a blanket from the shelf and spreads it over his patient's feet and thighs.

"Loosen your buttons if you will," he says. He pulls up Hari's shirt and after leaning forward places the stethoscope on his chest.

"I hear you saved our Catherine from doing herself some real harm the other day," Dr. Cotter says, moving back.

"That he did," Mr. Owens says, before Hari can reply.

"It would suit you if this boy never regained his memory, wouldn't it, Owens? He'd be around to save Catherine all the time then."

"Wouldn't wish that on the lad," Mr. Owens quickly says, his voice faltering.

Hari has a flash of memory: a somewhat similar—yet stronger—expression in another man's face, acute mortification at being caught out, naked shame. He strains unsuccessfully to recapture the specifics.

When Dr. Cotter is done examining his patient's back, he pats Hari's leg rather heavily and as he does so Hari lets out a pain-filled moan.

The doctor tosses off the blanket and edges up Hari's trousers. "What's this, then?" On Hari's right shin is a three-inch vertical gash, skin reddened around its periphery, greenish-yellow pus collected in its narrow crevice. Dr. Cotter leans down and sniffs. "Foul," he mutters, then gently palpates the skin around the gash. Hari lets out another moan. "It's warm to the touch," the doctor declares. "How long have you had this?"

Hari is silent.

"He fell into the river the day before yesterday. He must have hurt himself then," says Mr. Owens.

Dr. Cotter washes his hands at the corner basin. When he returns, he carefully cleans the wound bed and rotates a swab inside the crevice, keeping away from its edges. Afterwards, he applies an ointment and dresses the open gash. His touch is light in spite of his bulky fingers.

"The pain and fever will lessen in due course. But pay good heed: the healing cannot be rushed."

He provides Hari with some extra dressing, and a small

bottle of tablets and says to send for him if the fever gets worse. Hari pictures the Llandudno bus leaving without him, and as he and Mr. Owens walk back up the hill, he welcomes his aching shin as the only distraction to a sharp hopelessness that grows with every step.

~ FOUR ~

THE FOLLOWING MONDAY, Hari's temperature returns to normal. He offers to help Mr. Owens clear out the shed that the old man has decided to convert into a workplace; he wants to make his wooden horses within the earshot of Catherine. She has been keeping late hours at the day nursery, leaving the cottage before Hari is up, helping Eileen with the annual summer concert. Mr. Owens is attentive to her needs, making sure she eats a proper supper and takes her medicine before going to bed. Sometimes, Catherine's eyelids droop and her movements are disjointed and slow.

The next afternoon, Mr. Owens and Hari return from the village to find her in the kitchen, kneading dough. In spite of her pallor, she looks rested and alert. Mr. Owens is pleased that she is home early and tells her so repeatedly. Catherine turns to Hari and greets him shyly, her expression unnaturally coquettish. Mr. Owens gives her an appraising look and asks Hari to lend him a hand in the shed.

Later, when they are ready to eat, Hari moves to the table and like always, holds out a chair for her to sit on.

She glances up at him and asks why he looks so happy.

"Peter is going to Llandudno on Thursday and has offered to drop me off at the train station," he says.

"But I thought you were catching the Friday bus." Two red blotches appear on her cheeks.

"This way I will reach London a day earlier," Hari explains, confused by Catherine's adverse reaction.

Mr. Owens is watching them closely.

"It's Dawn's birthday tomorrow, and I promised I'd stay the night there," Catherine says.

"But what has that got to do with Hari's departure, pet?"

She ignores her father's question. "Well, I just won't go to the party then."

"That won't do, Catherine. Eileen has given you the day off so you can help her prepare for it."

"And why not? I'll send on with you the berry tarts and other savouries I promised."

Hari is confused. It is as if Mr. Owens and Catherine are speaking in code, and he cannot understand what they are saying.

Catherine leans towards him. "Leave on Friday as planned. Don't go on Thursday. Please."

Hari lays down his fork and stares at his plate. The pleading, the unhappiness, the disappointment feels acutely familiar, as does the sudden, unbidden memory of a woman's soft face against his own. A strong yearning triggered, he reaches for his water. His clumsy hand topples the glass; fortunately it is empty.

"Are you all right?" Mr. Owens asks.

Hari nods.

Mr. Owens turns to his daughter and says, "You can always pop down to the post office on Thursday morning, to see Hari off."

Catherine clutches the edge of the table and bestows on her father an uncharacteristically hateful look.

"Now that that's settled," Mr. Owens says in a quiet voice, ignoring her response. "Eat up and go to bed, pet. You look worn out."

Hari does not understand the strange current that is running between father and daughter; he excuses himself quickly and retires to his room.

The following morning Mr. Owens suggests that Hari visit the haberdashery in order to purchase some articles of dress. They make their way to the adjacent village on bicycles. The shelves in the shop are half-empty and Mr. Owens in an undertone suggests that since Hari has money but no coupons to buy clothes, he offer to overpay. Hari agrees. He sets aside two sets of underwear and socks, a pair of trousers, two shirts and a vest made of rough, warm wool. He asks the sales clerk whether she has any raincoats, but Mr. Owens urges Hari to take with him the one he has been wearing, along with the cap. "I never use them," he says, when Hari protests.

The shopkeeper, a small woman who has climbed a ladder to reach the upper shelves descends now, her arms laden with sweaters; she spreads them out in front of Hari. "Pure lamb's wool," she says.

The sweater Hari pulls forward is soft and patterned with diamonds in two shades of blue. He tells her he will take it.

Back at the cottage, Hari, who has treated Mr. Owens to an early ploughman's lunch, is feeling more optimistic by the minute; in less than twenty-four hours he will be far away from this isolated, cut-off world. Catherine appears to be in a better mood, too. She tells Hari that the berry tarts that she was baking that morning have turned out well and that she has just a few other items to prepare. Hari retreats to his room but can hear her flitting between the piano and the stove, playing short and long pieces as time and the cooking process permit. After a while, she knocks on Hari's door and asks with a demure smile whether there is any particular tune that he would like to hear.

"Not really," he says. "Play anything you like."

"Anything?" Her tone is bashful.

When he continues to lie down, she says, "Aren't you going to come and listen?"

He sets down his book and follows her into the sitting room.

He perches himself on the edge of the armchair and crosses his arms.

She lays her splayed fingers on the keys and extending her neck immerses herself in supple music that appears to reflect her mood. When the tune comes to an end, she looks up at him, her expression begging approval.

He claps half-heartedly just as Mr. Owens walks in. Taking in the scene, he strides across the room, and swiftly shuts the lid of the piano.

"But Pappy!" Catherine says, looking as though she might cry.

Mr. Owens fetches a pail from the kitchen and thrusts it into his daughter's hand. "If you could please lend me a hand in the shed?"

When they return inside, Mr. Owens reminds Catherine yet again that he has promised Eileen that she will be at her place no later than five o' clock to give Eileen a much-needed hand with the party preparations. He, Mr. Owens, will walk down with Catherine since he also has a five o' clock meeting with a gentleman who is coming in all the way from Llangollen.

At teatime, Catherine places in front of Hari two berry tarts. They are sweet and sharp on the tongue, and he wonders when he is finished them whether she can spare another. Cheeks reddening at the implied compliment she gives him two more. After the tea things are rinsed and put away, Mr. Owens opens the front door and asks Catherine whether she is ready to leave.

"Ready to leave?" she repeats. In spite of her father's earlier reminder, Catherine's tone is disbelieving.

"Hurry up, then."

"We've only just finished tea," Catherine says. "I still have to change my clothes."

"Well, hurry up," Mr. Owens says again. He returns his cap to the hook on the wall, and sits in the armchair.

"I don't know long I'll be."

Mr. Owens clucks his tongue in anger.

"But Pappy! I'm not finished yet. You keep your appointment and I'll run down to Eileen's as soon as I'm done."

Snatching his cap, Mr. Owens stomps out of the cottage, without bidding either of them goodbye.

Catherine goes up to her room.

A cold band is tightening around Hari's forehead. He wishes it were tomorrow already. The silent cottage where no one ever visits makes him long for something more, something he is as yet powerless to identify. A walk to the village green will no doubt clear his mind and help pass the time. But first, he will take a brief nap. He stretches himself on the cot in the kitchen and closes his eyes. Soon afterwards, he hears mincing footsteps. "*Me loukarach parat yayeen*," he says.

"In English, please!"

"I'll be back before you know it. *Me loukarach parat yayeen*."

Someone is shaking him by the shoulder. "Hari, wake up! You're talking in your sleep."

He feels Catherine's breath on his face even as he opens his eyes, and sitting up quickly he grabs the furled umbrella that he has propped against the cot.

"Where do you think you're going?" she says, moving forward and shutting the window to keep out the rain.

"For a walk."

"In this miserable weather?"

Without replying, he opens the door. Everything feels askew, imprecise; little black spots are dancing in front of his eyes.

"I'm almost ready," Catherine says, "Don't leave without me."

He stands in the doorway, his hand repeatedly warding off a giddy wasp that is hell-bent on dashing into him.

At long last, Catherine is done.

The drizzle has gained strength. He opens his umbrella and starts alone down the path.

"Aren't you going to walk me to Eileen's?" Catherine asks, catching up to him. She tosses back her hair that is held together with a green satin ribbon.

He looks at her blankly.

"Hari, are you all right?"

She holds out to him the basket containing the tarts, and he has no choice but to take it. "Won't you walk me to Eileen's?" she repeats.

"I won't be able to find my way back," he protests.

"Of course you will!" She points towards the rear of the house. "There's a short cut I know."

Knowing he ought to oblige her—the basket is heavy—he repeats, "I don't want to get lost."

"You won't. I promise. You'll be back in half an hour, maybe less." Eyes fixed over his left shoulder, she mouths something.

Hari turns around swiftly; there is no one there.

"Whom were you talking to?" he asks.

Catherine ignores his question.

Evidently, the invisible entity is back. Hari shivers as a cool breeze ruffles his hair.

The path is beaten and winds through an open meadow, and by the time they sight the village in the valley below, thunder is crackling and lightning is illuminating flaccid clouds. His umbrella dripping sheets of water, he follows Catherine into what appears to be an abandoned hut. He stands beside her at its narrow entrance and peers at the sky, the rain creating a muffled din as it crashes into the stone shelter.

Catherine steps back, away from a puddle that is growing at their feet and signals for him to follow her inside. The basket is getting heavier; he enters and sets it down at one end of a long table that stands underneath the mossy ceiling. He looks at Catherine. Her ribbon is askew and her damp hair hangs in ringlets around her face. Her eyes are glittering and her lips are slightly parted. Heart beating erratically, he immediately turns on his heel. He has almost reached the exit when Catherine comes around from behind him and standing on her toes, covers his mouth with her own. Confused, he pulls back sharply, his face a cold mask. Gripping the hands that are still latched onto the band of his trousers, he thrusts them away. Catherine lets out a moan and this time wraps her arms around his neck. He grabs her forearms in an attempt to pry them loose, but her hold is tight and her eyes are fervent, almost fanatical, and he is reminded of the evening when she came running into the cottage with blood from a self-inflicted wound trickling into her palm. Frightened by her illness, the thought of how she might adversely react to his rejection sends panic coursing down his body. Feeling impossibly trapped, his grip around her arms momentarily loosens, and Catherine right away leads him by the hand

and walks him back to the long table. She swings her legs up onto it and without releasing her grip on his shirt lies down and pulls him on top of her. He clamps shut his eyes, and when she is finished he picks himself up and stumbles into the rain, all at once furious and wretched with shame at his craven submission.

Catherine steps outside and they walk down the hill in silence. When Hari spots a wooden sign at the end of the lane with the name of Eileen's nursery painted across it, he stops and sets down the basket. "I think it's best we say goodbye here," he says, quickly adding the first thing that comes to mind: "I hope you get better soon." His tone is rigid and formal, and before he can raise his eyes, she is gone.

Early the next morning, Hari places a roll of money in the medicine cabinet; there's enough to cover the expense of his food and lodging, and then some. He waits by the rocking horse with trepidation, wondering whether Catherine has told her father about their encounter of the previous afternoon.

But when Mr. Owens enters the kitchen, he is whistling a pleasant tune. "I have a favour to ask of you," he tells Hari.

"No favour will equal what you have done for me."

"When you return to India, which one day you no doubt will, would you write my friend and ask him to send some medicine for Catherine? If you will pay him for his efforts, I'd be much obliged."

"Yes, of course."

"I knew I could count on you. I've already inserted Harold's name and address, and ours, in the inner pocket of that duffel bag." Mr. Owens points to the piano stool where he has placed the luggage. "On another piece of paper I have written the address of India House. As I told you last night, you have nothing to worry about. There are always hotels in and around the vicinity of railway stations and once you arrive in London find one and check into it. The following morning ask for directions at the front desk and go to India House. See whether you are registered there. If you are not registered, I am certain that someone at the House will be able to help you." He gives Hari an encouraging smile.

Once again filled with gratitude, Hari thanks Mr. Owens.

Before they exit the cottage together, his host hands Hari a shoebox. "Something to eat," he says. "It's a day's journey to London."

A scrappy sun is pushing through cloud as they walk down the hill. They don't have to wait long before Peter's van trundles to a halt.

"I wonder where Catherine is," Mr. Owens says. "She was at the piano all evening, granting everyone's requests.

She probably just overslept." He sounds relieved.

Before Hari can respond, Peter rolls down his window and calls out, "Let's get going."

Mr. Owens clasps Hari's hand in both of his and says, "I wish you all the best."

Hari swallows, not trusting himself to speak. Now that the eagerly anticipated moment has arrived, it isn't easy saying goodbye. He enters the van and leaning out of the window, waves his hand. Shameful thoughts of what transpired with Catherine rush into his mind but it is too late to offer a confession, or ask for her father's forgiveness.

He gazes up at the sky as Peter drives away and as the van picks up speed he almost misses Catherine standing in a dip by the side of the road. Her colourless face is tilted upwards and her hands are pressed low against her abdomen. He ducks his head; and when he looks up again, she is thankfully lost from sight.

Made uncomfortable by Catherine's unexpected decision to witness his departure, Hari is filled with dread that some unanticipated circumstance will prevent him from getting away. It is not until the sign for Llandudno comes into view that his heart quickens with relief. He thanks Peter for the ride and by the time they pull in beside the railway station, Hari can hardly wait to reach London.

He catches a train to Chester. The onward journey to London feels drawn out. To give himself something to do, he eats the lunch provided by Mr. Owens. It does nothing to settle the quiver of nerves; for the very first time since he lost his memory he is truly on his own. He closes his eyes and dozes restively, thoughts of Catherine prodding his conscience every time he jolts awake. How could he have been so cowardly? Why, on the very eve of his departure, did he allow himself to be seduced? His brain gnarled and knotted, he stares at his sombre reflection in the windowpane and by the time the train reaches its destination, the sky is dark and the city is filled with shadows.

He is the last to step out onto an empty platform and the ticket booth where he thought he might ask for directions is equally deserted. He walks into the street only to be met by a smell of charcoal and grime. Beyond the arches of the station there sprawls a junction in which dimmed traffic lights are blinking; street lamps are snuffed out and the windows and doorways of buildings have the appearance of blinded eyes. A double-decker bus slowly turns the corner, its headlights reduced to a slit. The single pedestrian waiting to cross the road steps forward in its wake, glancing cautiously to the left and right, his silhouette almost indistinguishable against the darkened street. An unseen clock emits nine loud gongs.

Hari walks down the street and enters the first hotel he encounters. The scent of the dark polished wainscotting evokes a rush of memory, and heart bursting with hope and anticipation, he checks himself in. He is shown into a carpeted chamber with heavy furniture. He runs a hot bath, sensing in a way he never has before that remembrance is just around the corner.

The room has turned colder and a weak sun is forcing its grey light through the edge of the curtain when he opens his eyes. He finishes washing up, then leaves his room and walks down the corridor that leads to the dining room. Pots of frangipani stand at its entrance, and no sooner do his eyes alight on the yellow-centred white flowers than he remembers the fragrant bushes that had lined the driveway to the guesthouse in Chikaldhara so many years ago.

He takes his seat at a table by the window, hiding his trembling mouth behind a hastily snatched napkin—for at last he knows who he is, how he came to be here, and why he should never have left Vasanti.

II

February 1942

NAGPUR, INDIA

~ FIVE ~

WHEN SHE WAS FIFTEEN, Vasanti woke up one morning with a full-fledged notion lodged inside her head: she would study beyond matriculation and play badminton just like her cousin, who had recently won a doubles championship in Poona's echoing gymnasium.

When she shared with her father her aspirations, Sitarampant, who lovingly gave every wish of his daughter weighted consideration, said, "Do you have a subject in mind?"

"English," Vasanti replied.

Sitarampant, who taught Marathi, Sanskrit and Mathematics in high school, was puzzled. "Why English?" he asked.

A frequent visitor to her uncle Vishnupant's residence in Bombay, Vasanti was envious that her uncle and his family spoke it so well. "That's why," she explained. "One day I want to be able to speak English fluently, just like them."

"And so you will," Sitarampant replied to his daughter. "As for badminton, I have an idea."

He requested that Vasanti help him clear their inner courtyard of the growth that had pushed up through crevices of the packed earth, and afterwards, alongside her spinster aunts—who had tended to her ever since the death of her mother some twelve years previously—she watched Sitarampant as he created a rough model of a badminton court using nails and corded rope. When that was done they waited for the rain to stop, and once the lines were painted in and the net hung up, Vasanti and her father played her very first game of badminton, underneath a pristine sky.

As for learning English, Sitarampant told her to be patient; one day, perhaps later than sooner, she would find the opportunity to fulfill what was in her heart.

For the next two years, Vasanti's was a reasonably carefree existence. Then, when she turned seventeen, her father took severely ill and was consequently forced to resign from teaching school. Two months into his ailment, early one August morning, Vasanti walked into his room with a cup of tea only to discover that she couldn't get him to wake. She called out to her aunts, and when the sight of his half-open eyes and slackened mouth became too much to bear, she kept watch on the high stool outside his window even as the doctor tried to revive him. When the man left, shaking his head, she continued to sit there, adamant in her refusal to believe that this indeed might be the end. It was when she was walking to the kitchen for a glass of water that a stertorous gasping perforated her ears, and by the time she ran back to her father's room, the last breath was leaving his body. After staring at his face, now peaceful and unlined, she extricated herself from her aunt's embrace, lowered her head onto his feet, and shuddered as sorrow encircled her in its unpitying grip.

That very afternoon, her brother Vinod, who was her elder by eleven years, travelled from Bombay to Poona, accompanied by their uncle, Vishnupant, and their cousin, Keshav. Upon seeing her distraught expression, all three attempted to reassure her that she was not alone, that the rest of the family would look after her and that all said and done, it was better that Sitarampant's illness had been short and that he had passed away peacefully. But no amount of consoling could blot out the fact that Vasanti would never again experience her father's hand on her forehead when it was time to wake in the morning; or wait for the sound of his returning footsteps so she could share with him all that had happened during her day. The pride with which he had explained to her his meticulous accounting; his devout evening prayers; the cross look he gave her aunts when they tried to serve him jackfruit; his patriotic fervour whenever he discussed independence from British rule—all these affectionate memories she shared with friends and relatives when they came by to pay their condolences, the tears leaking out of her eyes every time she pictured his loving face.

The prescribed thirteen days of mourning and religious ceremonies completed, her uncle, cousin and brother returned to Bombay. The ensuing weeks stumbled along in a strange and unfamiliar rhythm, and one afternoon in early November, Vasanti's aunts informed her of the family's decision to bring to a satisfactory conclusion a marriage proposal that had been sent by Sitarampant to the Chafékar family of Nagpur a couple of months prior to his death.

Her voice broken but defiant, Vasanti informed them that her father had made no mention of any such proposal. The aunts, instead of raising their voices, patiently explained that his silence was without doubt the result of his wasting disease: he simply had not had the energy to broach the topic.

"But he would have said something to me," Vasanti insisted.

Mai, her older aunt, said, "Perhaps he didn't wish to say anything because nothing was settled. The answer to Sitarampant's proposal came only in September, after he'd passed away."

"Why didn't you tell me this then?"

Bebitai, her younger aunt, walked over to Vasanti and, stroking her cheek, said, "We know how difficult these last couple of months have been for you. We didn't wish to rush things or bother you with something that had not yet been decided or fixed."

Her mind filling with hurt and anger, Vasanti extricated herself and stepped outside, as had become her habit in moments of despair. She picked up her badminton racquet and focused once again on practising her serves.

By the following morning, despite a sleepless night caused by the shock of receiving such unforeseen news, Vasanti's curiosity was nonetheless aroused. "What do you know about the Chafékar family?" she inquired of her aunts.

"Not much," Mai said, relieved that her niece had recovered from the sullen dejection of the previous day.

"Then at least tell me what their September letter said."

"Simply that they wished to pursue your father's proposal," Bebitai replied.

"So we sent all the correspondence along with your horoscope to your uncle Vishnupant and asked him to take over the communication started by Sitarampant."

"We heard from your uncle only yesterday." Mai pointed to the letter that was on the table behind her. "The boy's horoscope and yours are a match and his father and brothers have accepted you as a bride for Vijay."

"The marriage will take place as soon as an auspicious date is found," Bebitai added.

Vasanti's mouth trembled as she said, "What do you mean *as soon?*"

They were sitting in the veranda of the inner courtyard and Mai wrestled from Vasanti's hand the badminton racquet she was tightly gripping. Holding out a handkerchief, Mai said, "It's a good match, Vasanti. You know your father would have chosen only the very best for you."

"But I don't want to get married," Vasanti cried. "I don't want to leave Poona. And Nagpur is so far away."

"Don't you think we will miss you too?" Mai said. "Probably far, far more than you will miss us. But that's no reason to keep you by our side forever, is it?"

"Sooner or later you will have to get married," Bebitai said. "You don't wish to be a spinster, do you?"

"At least there are the two of us to keep each other company." Mai tried to convince her niece. "Who will you have?"

With this, they gave Vasanti the space to digest the changes that must follow, and as the days went by, sad as she was at the thought of marrying and leaving her maiden home and more than a little nervous when she contemplated the unknown future, in her heart Vasanti knew her aunts were carrying out her father's ultimate aspiration. Therefore, there was only one question that she asked her uncle when he arrived in Poona to inform them of the wedding date: "Is the boy educated?"

"He most certainly is," Vishnupant said. "Vijay—I am informed his relatives call him Baba—is a lawyer. His three older brothers, alongside their father, run the family business. The brothers are married to three sisters. The mother died a while ago. What else can I tell you?"

"Have you met the boy?" Vasanti asked.

Vishnupant shook his head. "But I met the boy's father, Nanasahib Chafékar, a couple of years ago, when he visited Bombay University to set up a scholarship for indigent students wishing to study history. In fact it was I who suggested to your father that he should consider Nanasahib's youngest as a prospective bridegroom for you."

"Then why didn't you say anything when you came here for Appa's funeral?" Vasanti asked.

Vishnupant looked at his niece. "I had no idea your father had responded to my suggestion until your aunts sent me all the correspondence. That wasn't until quite a bit later."

Mai said, changing the subject, "What more can you tell us about the Chafékars?"

And so Vishnupant launched into the story of how, in his inaugural speech for the scholarship, Nanasahib Chafékar had expanded upon the life of his deceased father, Raosahib, in whose name the fund had been set up. He explained to his audience that sometime in the late 1860s, after three years of continuous drought, Raosahib had left his family in Bhusawal and travelled west to Nagpur, determined to make his fortune in the cotton trade. Penniless, he had begun his career by buying and selling cloth on the street, and within five years, by dint of sheer hard work and austere behaviour, he had convinced a local merchant to forward him a loan. With this borrowed money, Raosahib purchased a small company called Surya Spinning Cotton Mills. This turned out to be a wise investment, for around the time the Mills came under Chafékar control, the American Civil War broke out, and there was a major disruption of cotton supplies. Before the war, only twenty percent of the world's cotton was exported from India, but with the blockade of American ports the price of Indian cotton rose and India began raking in several million sterling annually in the cotton trade.

"So you see, Vasanti," Vishnupant concluded, "my brother made a wise choice when he picked this boy for you. The Chafékars are a well-established, respectable, hard-working family, and believe me when I say that you will lack for nothing."

Bebitai was impatient now to know the wedding date set by the astrologer.

"February second," Vishnupant informed them.

"But that's so soon," Vasanti cried.

"You'll be all right, Vasru," her uncle said affectionately.

And over the following weeks, in order to soothe the panic that travelled around her gut every time she contemplated the imminent ceremony, Vasanti told herself to trust her uncle, that Baba was a lawyer, and that education in a husband was a superior thing, one that could only bode well.

Once, while she lay abed, she recalled the solitary words her father had spoken regarding the role of a wife. He had been telling her stories from the epic *Ramayana*. "Sita was the ideal consort," he'd said. "Pure, devoted, all-suffering and loyal. When Lord Rama was exiled from his father's kingdom, not wanting to see his wife suffer hardships in a forest full of unknown danger, he went to her chamber to take her leave. There he saw Sita dressed in a simple garb, stripped of the finery befitting a princess. And before he could bid her farewell, she told him that she was ready to accompany her Lord into the forest, adding, 'Wherever Rama goes, there goes Sita.'"

Tears filled Vasanti's eyes as she remembered her father's slow and thoughtful voice, full of love not only for the Divine Incarnate Lord Rama, but also for her.

Because the distance to Nagpur was several hundred miles, and the wedding date less than three months away, it was decided by Vasanti's uncle that there would be no formal engagement. Consequently, Vasanti first set eyes on her

husband, the twenty-four-year-old Baba, at the commence-
ment of the wedding rituals when the priests removed the
silk shawl that separated the bride from the groom. Too
shy to look into his face, Vasanti nevertheless noticed that
when she placed a garland of roses around his neck, he had
to bend considerably in order to enable her to do so. This
then was her initial impression of him: tall, with feet that
were lean, narrow and fair; and red knuckles that gripped
tightly the garland he would place around her neck.

During the ensuing ceremony in front of the fire,
emboldened by her curiosity, she wished to glance his way;
but, aware of vigilant eyes, she pinned her attention on the
dancing flames and watched them disappear into the invisible air. Later, when they were required to join hands, she did
so tentatively, and Baba must have shared her reluctance too
for he started to withdraw his fingers before the priest had
given him permission to do so.

After the religious rituals, she changed out of her gold-
embroidered sari into a simpler one and as she sat underneath
a spreading tree surrounded by the unfamiliar ladies of the
Chafékar clan, she whispered to her aunts seated on either
side of her, "Must you leave tomorrow?" It was a rhetorical
question; her aunts moved closer and said they hoped that
she would get an opportunity to visit them in Poona soon.

When Vasanti saw her bridegroom again, it was during
lunch; they were seated side by side at a long table. He did

not address her or turn her way, and was quiet and remote, except when his younger cousins approached him. He laughed and joked with them and gestured for the smallest to come nearer; the little boy crawled underneath the table and sat on Baba's lap and took from his uncle's hand the sweetmeat offered him. For her part, Vasanti kept her head bent and picked at her food steadily until everything on her silver plate was finished.

Soon, it was late afternoon. Surrounded once again by the women of her new family, all of them strangers making strange talk, amongst them her sisters-in-law who appeared to be about three or four years older than she, Vasanti glanced beyond the vestibule and caught herself staring directly into Baba's grey-blue eyes; so unexpected was this encounter that they both broke gaze instantly. And later, when she looked his way again, he was nowhere to be seen.

The reception was a whirr. She was introduced to a stream of well-wishers and even though, on account of war-time rationing, by Chafékar standards the celebrations were low-key and tame, there were scores of people milling around. Standing alongside Baba in front of the bridal thrones on a carpeted podium, Vasanti took surreptitious glances around the marquee. She recognized Baba's brothers, who appeared sociable and easy-going as they mingled with family and friends. The older two, Suresh and Ramesh, did not resemble Baba at all, for they were short and squat with dark complexions and fleshy necks. Yogesh, the youngest, was tall with sloping shoulders.

Nanasahib, Baba's father, had visited the bride's party at their rest house the previous evening, and had addressed Vishnupant with such elegant charm that Vasanti had taken to him right away. He was seated now at the farthest end of the marquee, surrounded by a group of distinguished men, one of whom wore a turban with a diamond and ruby brooch.

Daunted by all this privilege, not to mention the prospect of sharing the house with so many people, Vasanti looked around for her sisters-in-law. Amita and Nina were attending the refreshment table; and the oldest, Sheela, was walking towards them. She held out a couple of bowls, and giving Vasanti and Baba a sympathetic smile, said, "Now that everyone has greeted you, there's no need to keep standing. Here, eat this ice cream before it melts."

Late at night, after the guests had departed and Vasanti had bid her maiden relatives a tear-filled goodbye, Sheela escorted her up a single flight of stairs to a large chamber. It was well furnished and had two anterooms adjoining it.

Walking forward, Sheela drew the curtains across the windows, then, turning to Vasanti, said, "Baba should be up soon." And after giving the newest Chafékar member an encouraging smile, she left, closing the door behind her.

Heart beating awkwardly, Vasanti surveyed her surroundings: the bedroom slippers ready and waiting for Baba's large feet; the cluttered desk stacked with law books; the open French doors leading into the terrace beyond; and the single, wooden four-poster bed, linens turned down for the night, ready for occupation. Tears of shock choking her breath, she mentally chastised her aunts for failing to inform her that she would be sharing quarters with Baba and not with the women of the household, as she had done in Poona. Relaxing her clenched jaws she absent-mindedly repeated her father's favourite prayer: *Grant me Courage, O Lord and Grace, and the most valuable virtue of all, Patience.*

She walked towards the anterooms, one of which was lined with overflowing bookshelves and the other with a dressing table and full-length mirror, reflecting wardrobes that stretched from ceiling to floor. She leaned against the open terrace door, a nervous lump forming inside her throat, and stood there a long time, staring at the fractured image of the pitted moon in the water below, and just as her eyes were beginning to droop, for it had been a long and exhausting day, she heard the click of a door latch. Wondering whether she was expected to acknowledge Baba's presence, she stayed where she was; and it wasn't until he had pulled down the metal chain of his bedside lamp that she faced him.

~ SIX ~

BABA SWITCHED ON THE LIGHT and the girl turned towards him and stood there rigid, dressed in her wedding finery, one arm leaning against the door jamb, the other limp by her side. He had managed to avoid her all day, and now that they were alone, he was annoyed that he would no longer be able to do so.

He acknowledged her presence with a nod, and she right away said, "In Poona, the water tank is far away. Not like this, within sight." She spoke pedantically, as though the words issuing from her mouth had been well rehearsed.

"It's a swimming pool," he said, discarding his shoes. He slipped his feet into the bedroom slippers.

"Do you swim?" Her voice was low-pitched, with just the hint of a tremble.

"No."

She swiftly dropped her eyes.

Embarrassed by his abruptness and despite his resolution not to engage her in conversation, he said, "Have you had a chance to walk around the grounds?"

"We came from Poona only yesterday."

"Who else came with you?"

"My aunts, of course." She sounded surprised that he would not know. "And my brother and his family from Bombay. And my uncle Vishnupant and his son, Keshavdada."

The memory of meeting her uncle and cousin was strong, but he couldn't recall the others. He started to move towards the dressing room, but when she kept standing there, her expression courteous and respectful, he once again felt compelled to address her.

"Aren't you going to change?"

"I don't know where my clothes are."

He lifted his chin. "Did you check in there?"

"No."

She followed him into the dressing room, keeping her distance.

"Your wardrobe is on the left side," he said, opening its door.

A quick glance showed him that her clothes had been placed within; there were very few of them. He gathered his pyjamas from the clotheshorse and entered the bathroom.

When he came out, she was sitting on the stool in front of the dressing table, her back to the mirror, a night sari and towel placed across her lap. Standing up, she held out a bunch of keys.

"Sheelatai told me to put all the jewellery in the safe but I can't get it to open."

He took the keychain and explained the sequence in which the keys ought to be inserted.

Turning away from him, she fiddled with the lock, and while she was struggling, he quickly ran his fingers over the jewellery she had placed on the dressing table: the warmth of her body had transferred itself to the gold. He waited for the door of the safe to click open before returning to the bedroom.

She was a long time changing, and when she appeared in the doorway dressed in a simple cotton sari, she looked much younger than her eighteen years. Her wrists were enclosed in gold and green glass bangles, her neck in a black-beaded mangalsutra, and her long hair had been combed out of its bun and loosely plaited for the night. He sat forward in bed and pulled up the quilt to cover his waist.

She went and leaned against the terrace door, which was now shut.

"Aren't you tired?" he said after a moment or two.

"I'm waiting for the servant to make up my bed."

"Your bed?"

"Yes," she said. "You are sleeping in yours and I suppose the servant will come by to make one up for me on the floor."

There was an extended silence. "Vasanti." Uttering her name felt strange and he stumbled through it. "This is also your bed." He pointed vaguely to the side that was unoccupied. Discomfort and confusion crossing her face, she nevertheless moved forward and sat at its edge, then drew up her feet and lying down, faced the wall.

Baffled by her childlike naïveté, Baba was more than a little relieved that she had no expectations for the wedding night. A few months ago, when he had precipitately made up his mind to study in England, he'd had no idea that his brothers and father had already accepted Vasanti as his prospective bride. Furious that they had not consulted him before finalizing the match, he had vehemently aired his objection. And when his brothers dismissed it, he told them that he would marry the girl upon his return. He had even offered to have the engagement ceremony before leaving Nagpur. But Vasanti had only recently lost her father and was orphaned, his oldest brother had said, and her uncle therefore would not be likely to consider any postponement. Since the Chafékar family had given its word and there was no plausible recourse, Baba had had little choice but to agree to the February wedding date. Now, watching Vasanti, he wished yet again that he had insisted his brothers inform her family prior to the wedding that in a few months' time he was planning to be gone.

Looking again at Vasanti's dainty shoulders and the braided hair that lay against her back in a silken rope, he reminded himself why he must keep his distance. His definite plans to set sail for England in the midst of a war that continued to claim countless lives brought up the possibility that he might never return. It was unwarranted and unjust to strike up an alliance that could well end in an ugly way.

Attempting to work inside his head excuses for when Vasanti was perhaps less exhausted and ready to stake her marital claim, he fell asleep—his last thought a previously unencountered suspicion that following through with his ascetic plan would require every ounce of his determination.

An oblong clock, its brass pendulum caught in the glare of the advancing sun, was blinking at Vasanti when she awakened the following morning. She threw aside her quilt and sat up in bed. Wasn't it always her practice to be up before dawn? Her very first morning at Chafékar Wadi and she had slept in: Whatever would her new family think? She turned her head: Baba was sprawled on his back, nightshirt rucked halfway up his chest.

Discomfited by his nearness and relieved that he was still sleeping, she hurried into the bathroom, and it was only after she was ready and dressed for the day that it occurred to her that she had no idea what to do next.

Baba was now turned in bed, and so as not to disturb him, she tiptoed towards the terrace and parted the window curtains to peer out at her new surroundings; and when the novelty of iridescent swooping birds dipping their beaks into the swimming pool wore off, she softly opened the bedroom door and walked down the stairs. All was quiet. The servants must have been up all night, for the large entrance hall and the carpeted drawing rooms beyond were spotless; the wooden floors were once again gleaming and polished; and but for the marquee that showed through the window, no one would have guessed that a wedding party had thronged the house the previous day. Shocked by all this efficiency and enchanted anew by the stateliness of her new home, she wished yet again that her father had lived long enough to see her settled in it.

Wandering down an open corridor in the direction where she imagined the kitchen to be, she stopped for a moment to breathe in the loamy and fecund scent of newly watered earth. Raising her eyes to the elliptical island of flowers opposite the front entrance, she noticed a car pulling out of the driveway.

She would have walked right past the dining room had her sisters-in-law not called out to her. They were wearing their night saris, and on the table in front of them were plates of dried fruit, biscuits and two pots of tea. As they regarded her, she was once again struck by how similar they looked:

each had the same narrow jaw and wheat-coloured complexion and their eyebrows were heavy-set and well defined. It was only in their eyes that they differed. Sheela's were round and thin-lidded whereas Nina's were myopic, with a tendency to squint. Amita's were watchful, her gaze flitting across faces, doling out verdicts, or so it seemed. The sisters greeted Vasanti enthusiastically and asked how the night had gone.

"I slept only towards the early morning," she replied. "I didn't mean to be up so late."

"That's only to be expected," Amita said, stifling a smile.

"Even if you hadn't appeared until noon, I daresay you would have been forgiven," Nina said.

"Forgiven?"

"They're only teasing you." Sheela poured Vasanti a cup of tea. "Here, you must be thirsty."

Vasanti reached for the cup but refused the proffered biscuit.

"Is Baba up?" Sheela asked.

"He was moving in bed when I came downstairs."

Sheela pushed a button on the wall. A few moments later she gave the summoned servant instructions to carry Baba's tea up to him, and asked whether tea had been delivered to the other rooms. The boy nodded and left.

Nina turned to Vasanti. "Sheelatai was saying that we must do our best to acquaint you with the ways of this household."

"That way you won't feel so lost," Sheela explained.

"Is there anything in particular then, that you would like to know?" Amita said.

Vasanti shrugged, not imagining where to begin.

"You can ask us anything," Amita urged.

"I saw a car just now, making its way towards the gate," Vasanti said.

"That must have been our father-in-law," Nina said, stirring her tea.

"Nanasahib lives at Pegasus," Amita added. "That's his stud farm."

"Stud farm?"

"His favourite hobby is horse breeding, so Pegasus is where he mostly resides. The stables are an hour north of Chafékar Wadi."

Fascinated by the idea that her father-in-law owned horses, Vasanti asked, "Have you been there?"

"No," Nina said. "Nobody ever visits Nanasahib at his farm. Whenever he has meetings in Nagpur, or family functions to attend, he comes to the Wadi and sometimes stays a night or two, depending on his work."

Vasanti felt relieved that there would be one less person to contend with, one less to get to know.

"I understand all of you were married together in a single ceremony?"

"Yes," Nina replied.

There was a short silence, after which Amita said, "What else can we tell her?"

Nina wiped her mouth with a napkin. "Today everything is running late and I don't know whether the men will go to work, but normally all four brothers leave the house between eight and nine in the morning. Our husbands go to the Mills and Baba goes to his law office. Sometimes, he attends High Court with his uncle Bhikumama, who is a district judge."

"Six-thirty, seven, other times as late as eight in the evening, they all return," Amita said. "So during the day there are only three—now four—of us who have the run of the Wadi."

"The house is well staffed so there's not too much for us to do," Nina said.

"Except when it comes to keeping accounts," Sheela reminded her. "Unfortunately, that's my headache. The accountant is a perfect martinet and demands that each and every naya paisa be entered and accounted for."

Amita said, "When we first came here we noticed that the cooks were lazy and not very sanitary because there was no lady of the house to supervise them."

"They're fine now," Sheela said.

"When did our mother-in-law pass away?" Vasanti asked.

"Quite some time ago, right after Baba finished his matriculation exam. Of all the sons, he was the closest to her, or so I've heard." It was evident from Sheela's voice that she held a soft spot for her youngest brother-in-law.

"Our pet name for your husband is Angrezi babu," Amita said. "We always tease him."

"He doesn't mind," Nina was quick to add.

"Why Angrezi babu?" Vasanti said.

"Because he's such an English-man," Amita replied. "You'll discover that soon enough."

Vasanti was puzzled.

"He likes everything British," Nina said. "You should see him when he attends formal dinners. Sometimes he wears a bow tie, other times a cravat."

"And he has a couple of light woollen suits that are made in England." Sheela pointed to the glass-fronted tall-boy. "See that dinnerware?"

Vasanti looked at the gilt-edged porcelain.

"All made in England. He purchased that set a few years ago."

"He's an anglophile, Vasanti," Amita said, setting down her teacup.

Nina chuckled and her sisters smiled, their amusement not at all unkind. Vasanti wished she knew as much about Baba as did her sisters-in-law.

"Since you are already bathed and dressed, why don't you walk around the grounds before it gets too hot?" Nina said.

Vasanti would have preferred instead to learn more about Baba, but the women were already pushing back in their chairs. She followed them out of the dining room.

At the front entrance, Nina pulled an umbrella from a brass container and thrusting it into Vasanti's hand, said, "Just so you don't spoil that beautiful fair complexion."

Vasanti blushed at the compliment.

As soon as Nina shut the door, a feeling of isolation engulfed her. She stood looking around for several minutes, not knowing where to go, when all at once she remembered the temple that she had been taken to at the start of the wedding ceremonies, the previous day. It was at the farther end of the compound. She started walking towards it now, making her way around the marquee, steering clear of the men who were taking it down, and it wasn't too long before she saw the saffron flag at its tapering summit. She passed underneath the stone lintel and after ringing the heavy brass bell that was suspended from the ceiling, joined her palms in front of Lord Shiva. Lit oil lamps caressed with steady light His serene face. She got down on her knees and touching her forehead to the ground, recited a Sanskrit prayer. Afterwards, she sat back on her haunches and thanked Him for a husband who did not have thick ears or a hairy nose and who possessed all his teeth. Her thoughts meandering, she envisioned Baba as he had stood next to her at the reception, strikingly handsome in a grey silk suit, greeting and acknowledging guests with quiet charm, asking Sheela with a mischievous smile to fetch him yet another bowl of ice cream. Getting to her feet, she continued to voice her gratitude, thanking Lord Shiva for her sisters-in-law, who had welcomed her in such a kind and thoughtful way. She concluded her prayers with an earnest entreaty that she would not miss her aunts too much, or her old home, and that she would indeed visit Poona before the end of the year.

She rang the temple bell once again, and before she could move away, the priest, Guruji, walked in through the back door. He had a round solemn face and wore thick glasses and she remembered him from the ceremonies of the previous day. He told her that the early morning was a good time to ask for Shiva's blessing, and after removing a sweetmeat from a silver bowl, he centred it on her palm. She placed it in her mouth and left, stopping to rinse her hands at the washbasin outside.

After taking leave of Guruji, she started back towards the house, following the path along the compound wall that skirted the outlying jungle. Running her fingers against the meshed wire fence on the other side of which ran a man-made canal, she thought yet again of her sisters-in-law, and even though in the temple she had been grateful for their welcoming and friendly natures, she admitted now that their closeness, the looks they darted each other, all made her feel like the newcomer she was.

Leaning her forehead against the wire fence she allowed the tears to course down her cheeks, and after collapsing the umbrella, she used its pointed end to score *I want to go home* into the moist soil at her feet. Much later, when self-pity was spent and she could cry no more, she knelt down and rubbed out the words she had written there. Lifting her head she stared at the reflecting water of the canal, and imagined her father urging her to brace herself. *Be practical*, the voice said, *and make a list of the various things you could do to settle in.*

It wasn't long before she came up with a few: She would ask her sisters-in-law to show her the family albums that she'd noticed were in the glass-fronted cabinets in the vestibule downstairs. This would help her get acquainted with the numerous members of the Chafékar clan. And not right away, but sometime soon, she would petition Sheelatai to take her by the High Court to see the building where Baba spent a portion of his day. The last request was without doubt the dearest to her heart and she hesitated to name it even to herself. An outdoor badminton court stood next to the temple: she wondered how her sisters-in-law would respond if she were to ask them to join her in a game.

Sun bouncing off walls and terraces, the white-washed buildings of Chafékar Wadi lay before her in all their expansive glory. Scrubbing her dried tears with the end of her sari, she approached the main house via the tennis court and went upstairs, hoping to enter an empty room. A servant boy was sweeping the floor; Baba was nowhere in sight, and his bedroom slippers were once again by his desk.

"I left Babasahib's ironed clothes on the window ledge in the dressing room," the boy said.

"What ironed clothes?" she asked.

"Six o' clock every evening Sahib goes horse riding," the boy replied. "Should the driver take the clothes to the club as usual?"

"I suppose so," she said.

"Sheela Bai told me to tell you that they are all at breakfast."

She went downstairs and trained her eyes on the floor in case she were to encounter a husband, including her own, and was relieved to see that once again, only her sisters-in-law were seated around the table.

"Come, Vasanti," Sheela said. "We're waiting for you. The men have eaten and left." She reached for the covered platter and after serving everyone their breakfast, passed around cups of tea.

Vasanti drained a glass of water, then another.

"Are you all right?" Nina asked, looking at her closely.

"I'm fine." She swallowed the tears that were again threatening to rise.

"What did you think of the grounds?" Sheela said.

"They are beautiful, and so very big."

"Where the marquee is being taken down is actually a cricket pitch," Nina said. "Almost every month there is a friendly cricket match."

"Between whom?" Vasanti asked.

"The four brothers and all the cousins and their numerous friends," Nina answered. "We always watch from the covered part of the terrace upstairs."

After a brief silence, Vasanti said, "I went to the temple. Guruji was there."

"Ramabai, our late mother-in-law," Sheela said, "had the temple erected soon after the family moved here."

"So Nanasahib built Chafékar Wadi?"

Amita shook her head.

Sheela said, "Baba was very small, I believe, when Nanasahib purchased Chafékar Wadi from the members of a private club. Before they moved here, the family lived in a modest house somewhere in the vicinity of the Mills. Once, I overheard our father-in-law say that Baba brought much luck to the family because it was only after his birth that the Chafékars rose to such prominence." There was pride in her voice.

Gordon Square, before Nanasahib bought it, was a Whites-Only club, her sisters-in-law explained to Vasanti over breakfast. Built a couple of decades before the turn of the century by British ex-patriots of middle income, the club had done well at first, but when some of its founding members chose to retire to England and several others got conscripted and dispatched abroad during the 1914 war, the membership had dwindled and suddenly there weren't enough funds to keep the establishment running. Nanasahib came to hear of its troubles from a business associate and offered to purchase the property. But before the deal was finalized, the former Secretary of the Club, a certain Mr. Watson, asked Nanasahib whether he could continue to rent the cottage that stood at the southern end of the premises. Nanasahib, who did not anticipate the use of that extra space, said he could.

"I don't think I saw that cottage," Vasanti said.

"You can't see it from here. It's in the opposite direction from the temple."

Overcome by nostalgia for the humble yet loving circumstances of her maiden home, Vasanti recalled with fierce affection the disciplined, lonely life of her beloved father; and remembering their penny-pinching ways, she felt an urgent need to be reunited with her well-meaning aunts.

"I think you're about to cry," Sheela said, leaving her chair and going to Vasanti's side.

Vasanti sat still to keep her eyes from overflowing.

"You'll be all right. There were three of us and yet it took us a while to settle in," Nina said.

In spite of all the empathy and perhaps because of it, Vasanti burst into tears, burying her face in her hands.

"Let her cry," Amita said, with a touch of cynicism. "After all, it's only her first day of married life."

That night after dinner, Baba sat up alone on his side of the bed. As was his habit, he opened the newspaper and scanned the items he hadn't had time to read during the day. Complete autonomy for India was once again in the news and the freedom fighters were divided in their opinion whether or not to support the Allies in their war effort against the Nazis. Subhas Chandra Bose had declared his backing for the Axis powers. Baba didn't agree with him. He felt it was important to apply pressure to get the British to leave, but he did not support the idea of joining an army that was fighting Great Britain; after all, India was still an integral part of the Empire.

There was a feeble knock on the door. He guessed it was Vasanti and told her to come in. She acknowledged him with a brief nod and disappeared into the dressing room. Emerging much later, she propped up the pillows on her side of the bed without looking at him. Swinging up her legs, she leaned back for a moment, only to sit forward in order to reach for the water on the table next to her. She took a small sip, afterwards replacing her glass carefully, and brought forward her plait so that it cupped one side of her face. She sat back patiently, perhaps waiting for him to switch off the lamp before lying down.

He was watching her from the corner of his eye.

She glanced his way and pointing towards the anteroom, said, "All those books . . . Have you read each and every one of them?" Again, that low voice glistening with naive wonder.

"Not quite, but I've read many of them, yes."

She pulled her quilt all the way up to cover her neck.

Deciding to ignore her, he raised his newspaper, but when she did not turn away, he said, "There are novels in that room. Poetry books, biographies, travelogues too."

"Are there history books?"

"Yes. Do you like history?"

She nodded, and before lying down and turning onto her side said, "My uncle teaches history at Bombay University."

"I didn't know."

She faced him again and, looking down, smoothed the tassels of her quilt. "It seems you don't know too much about me." Her voice was just above a whisper.

It was the very first time he was seeing her this close. Her small triangular face was as smooth as marble, as was her wide forehead and angled jaw; her lips were pink and slightly lush and barely discernible freckles peppered her high cheekbones. All this he registered in one great sweep, before she could raise her chin and train on him those luminous eyes. He wondered what she would do if he reached out and weighed with one hand the thick hair that fanned her breast. Her guileless expression told him that no similar thoughts were crossing her mind. And unexpectedly, there came to him a remark an aunt had made a long time ago, when he was a boy of seven, perhaps six.

There was a discussion amongst the women gathered in the terrace regarding the attributes of beauty. When no one named his mother as someone who so obviously possessed them all, he declared his Aai was without doubt the most beautiful person in the world. The women laughed, and an aunt pinched his cheek and said, "Your father was fortunate enough to find one such as Ramabai, and mark my words, Baba, one day you will marry a remarkable beauty too."

Now that Vasanti was facing him again, he found himself asking, "Did you go through the books on the shelves?"

She was silent.

"Well, did you?"

"I wouldn't touch your things without asking you first. Besides, they are all in English."

"So?"

"I don't know English."

He set aside the newspaper. "Nobody taught you?"

"I went to a Marathi medium school."

"I thought even Marathi medium schools taught some English."

"My school didn't." Her tone was defensive.

"But it's very important that you know how to speak it."

Looking down, she fiddled with the end of her plait.

After a pause he said, "If I were to teach it to you, would you be willing to learn?" And even as he uttered these words, he knew how reckless they were. He didn't know the first thing about tutoring, and most importantly, come July he was planning to be gone.

"I'd like that," Vasanti said, and as she smiled, two dimpled crescents appeared on either side of her mouth. Before he could retract his words, she asked, "When can we begin?"

He fumbled for an answer. "I don't know—I don't have the time, at least not for a long while."

Swallowing her disappointment, she said, "I always wanted to learn English."

"Then why didn't you?"

"After I passed matriculation, my father said he would get me a tutor. Then he took ill and he—we ran out of time." Her chin trembled but she controlled herself, and with a sudden change in conversational direction said, "Amita told me they call you Angrezi babu. Nina said you don't mind."

"She's right," Baba said. "I don't."

"Then it would be nice for you if I knew some English, would it not? I've always wanted to learn it and you just now said it's important that I know how to speak it. So why not teach it to me?"

The logic of her argument was faultless and once again he found himself bridging the distance that before their wedding he had been so keen to maintain. July and England were five months away. He would teach her a bit, as much as she was willing to learn; after that it would be up to her to make progress, or not.

"I'm free tomorrow evening. Be ready around seven-thirty. We'll sit at my desk."

She shut her eyes, perhaps to signal assent, perhaps to muffle her delight, then turning on her side she faced the wall.

Baba opened his newspaper and refocused his attention on the affairs of the world. When he couldn't concentrate, he said, "I'm not such a fatty, you know, that I need so much space. If you move away any farther you will fall off the bed and then what will you do?"

She made a show of shifting back towards him and he imagined the sides of her mouth breaking into those remarkable dimples. Without meaning to, he tossed the paper on the floor and switched off the lamp. Why was he being so friendly? What was the point in furthering a relationship that he would one day break? Nothing had changed: getting admitted to the bar at the Inns of Court was still a priority.

Gratified once again that she was keeping to her side of the bed, he told himself to confine their English lessons to merely that: teaching and learning. There was no need for affable chatter. That way when it was time to say goodbye, they would part company without harbouring disappointment, or feeling regret.

~

The day dragged slowly in anticipation of what was to come and at seven o' clock Vasanti was at Baba's desk, mopping with the end of her sari the little dust that had settled on its surface, tidying the stray sheaves of correspondence, restacking his law books to free up space. She was running her hand over the silver dragon paperweight when Baba walked in.

"I already filled the inkwell," she said.

"Can I bathe at least, and get out of my riding clothes?"

She saw his Jodhpurs were dusty and his shirt was patchy with sweat, and she blushed, embarrassed by her eagerness.

After he was bathed and changed, he entered his library and returned with a bound volume. "My favourite poems," he said, and pointing to the adjacent chair, motioned for her to take a seat.

He searched his desk drawer and after removing a brand-new notebook, wrote across its first page in a rapid yet well-formed hand. Holding up what he had written, he said, "Do you recognize this?"

"It's the alphabet."

"So you do know some English."

"I recognize the script as being English. And what else could it be?"

She saw him suppress a smile before handing her the notebook along with a pencil.

"I'm going to tell you how the alphabet is pronounced. I will go slowly because under each of those letters I have written on the page, I want you to write down in Marathi script the pronunciation of that letter."

She listened carefully and wrote neatly, and after that was done, he asked that she memorize the page. She closed her eyes and rocked backward and forward in her seat, intent on absorbing the very first lesson.

By the end of the half hour, she could pronounce without referring to her notes the first ten letters, *a* to *j*. Her head throbbing with concentration and now frustration that her brain had stopped functioning, she stared at the unlearned alphabet and prayed that he would bring their English lesson to a halt. As though reading her mind, he clicked shut his poetry book and looked at the clock. Saying she had learned enough for the day, he dismissed her.

She hurried to the bathroom and bolted the door. Sitting on the stool, she rotated her head in an effort to relax it: Whatever had she been thinking? That English was easy to learn? That merely wanting something is halfway to achieving it?

There was a knock on the door.

"You're not crying, are you?"

"Of course not!" she said, swallowing her tears.

She waited for Baba's footsteps to recede, and after a couple of minutes exited the dressing room only to see him on her side of the bed, a deadpan expression on his face. Before she could figure out why he was sitting there, he gave her an encouraging wink, and as she contemplated snatching a pillow, knowing that she wouldn't have the nerve to hurl it, he was gone from the room. She sat down in the depression caused by his body and fell back, laughing.

Later, when she went downstairs, the brothers were seated at the dining table. Her sisters-in-law, as at breakfast that morning, were once again in attendance, supervising the bearers as they served food. Upon seeing her, Sheela came forward and asked in an undertone how the English lesson had gone. Vasanti clutched her temples and rolled her eyes.

"Mark my words," Sheela said, smiling. "You will be the one to draw Baba out of his shell."

The brothers were engaged in business talk now and as she went forward and replenished their glasses with drinking water, Vasanti noticed that Baba had yet to say a single word.

After the men were done eating and the table had been set anew, the women sat down to dinner. By the time they went upstairs it was after ten o' clock.

Vasanti knocked on her bedroom door before entering. Baba was at his desk.

"Don't wait up for me," he said. His indifferent tone did not match the mood of his earlier wink.

Puzzled, she kept quiet and walked into the terrace only to see her brothers-in-law at its farther end, seated on cane chairs they must have pulled forward from a stack against the wall. She turned around and was about to step back into her room when they stopped talking and Yogesh, the youngest, pointed towards the far corner in the direction of a mounted instrument and said, "See that telescope? You might want to look at the stars."

So as not to appear rude, she walked to the stone balustrade and looked through the lens, scouting the amplified moon surrounded by an unmoving sky. The men continued to talk about market shares and labour issues, and when she thought they'd forgotten her presence, she returned to her room.

She retrieved her notebook from the desk and sat on the bed, and after going over the alphabet for the third time, addressed Baba's back: "To whom are you writing?"

"A friend."

"What friend?"

Without turning around, he said, "Christopher Watson."

"Who lives on the property?" There was surprise in her voice. "Sheelatai pointed out their cottage to me this morning."

He swivelled in his chair. "Only his father lives there now. Christopher moved to London a while ago."

"You have a British friend?"

"Aren't you sleepy?" His tone was dry and dismissive.

She pretended not to notice. "It's just that I've never met an English person before . . . and if I were to, I doubt we'd find anything in common."

"That's absolutely not true," Baba said. "Other than the colour of their skin and hair they are the same as us, you know."

"My father said that the British are different from us in every way." She pulled up her legs and sat cross-legged on the bed.

"*Every* way?"

"That's what he said and I believe him."

"And you don't believe me?"

"You will have to tell me about your British friend before I can answer that."

Clearly annoyed that they were once again engaged in conversation, he said, "I don't have to tell you anything."

Face blanching, she made for the dressing room.

"Maybe I'll tell you about Christopher some other time," he said.

She paused to take note of his conciliatory tone but didn't think it necessary to turn around. Confused that one minute he seemed to like her and the next he didn't, she shut the dressing room door and removed her night sari from the clotheshorse.

~ SEVEN ~

EACH DAY THE FOLLOWING WEEK, before Baba left for work, Vasanti asked him whether he would be back in time for their evening lesson; she seemed pleasantly surprised when he always said, "Yes."

Ten days into his pledge, upon waking one morning, Baba sat up in bed and before she could ask him, raised his voice and said, "Vasanti, seven-thirty as usual this evening. And be prepared to recite the alphabet, backward this time." He could see in the dressing room mirror her quick smile and was pleased that his mildly amusing remark had elicited such a sweet response.

She was an early riser, leaving their bed before sunrise while Baba was still fast asleep. The one time when he was awake before her, he pretended not to be. Through half-shuttered eyes he saw her open the terrace door cautiously, all the while glancing at the bed to make sure that he was not being disturbed. Then, enveloped by the cool morning air, she lifted her eyes and folded her hands in homage to the rising sun that was flooding the terrace in shades of pink. Reaching behind, she brought forward her long plait and unbraided the thick, wavy strands, afterwards running her hands through the tangled filaments to loosen the knots. And when her fingers encountered no obstruction, she entered the dressing room, and sitting in front of the mirror, tipped oil into her cupped palm and massaged it gently into her hair. He leaned forward in bed silently, and watched her flushed reflection, forehead beaded with the effort of combing out the unruly locks that required several hairpins to tame them into a neatly coiled twist.

Most days he would come awake long after she had groomed her hair. He would wait in the dressing room for his turn to use the bathroom, trying to ignore the fact that he was finding her more and more beautiful with each passing day. She would emerge fully dressed, a surprising and nimble feat: the bathroom floor was always flooded with water, and yet her sari was never wet. Shyly, and not meeting his gaze, she would turn to the mirror to apply the red kunku to her forehead, and by the time he had performed his ablutions, she would be sitting on the sofa in the nook next to the desk, ready and waiting to pour out two cups of tea.

They spent that first half hour of each morning together, he going through his briefcase and arranging his papers for the day and Vasanti watching the still denseness of the jungle reflected in the flowing canal. The parrots had made a guava tree by the swimming pool their favourite place to be and she would track them with her eyes as they scattered out of swinging branches, chattering and squawking, the green of their wingspan apparent, the red of their beaks too small to see.

Once, she said, "Parrots remind me of Poona."

"Do you miss Poona?' Baba asked.

She nodded.

"A lot?"

"Sometimes."

"It's been three weeks since you came to Nagpur."

"It will be three the day after tomorrow."

"It's too bad then that you haven't settled in yet."

"But I have," she was quick to correct him.

The tear-filled corners of her eyes belied her words and that night, when the air was uncommonly hot, making it difficult to sleep, Baba, convinced that it was time to reward Vasanti for all the effort she had been putting into her English lessons, said, "Are you awake?"

She immediately raised herself on her elbows. "Can I fetch you anything? Some water perhaps?"

"You asked me about Christopher some time ago. Are

you still interested in knowing how we became friends?"

"Of course I am," she said.

"There's quite a bit to relate, so I'll tell you as much as I can tonight."

She sat up and faced him cross-legged on the bed.

"Christopher was born in that cottage Sheela pointed out to you the first week, except the property was called Gordon Square then."

"I know. Sheelatai told me how Nanasahib purchased the estate when you were very little."

Baba went on to explain that it was around the time he turned ten that Christopher and his older sister, Susan, started to pass the house at the same time every evening, right when the Chafékar boys and their friends would be playing cricket in the clearing next to the tennis court. Invariably, Christopher would get the driver to toot the car horn and the players would stop their game and wave to the grinning boy, who would be sticking his head out of the car window while shouting out incomprehensible cheers. So obviously was he a fanatic of the game that it was automatically assumed—without any shred of proof—that whenever a red season ball went missing from the shed, it was the Watson boy who had stolen it.

One November, a few years later, when family and well-wishers had congregated at Chafékar Wadi to celebrate Baba's fourteenth birthday, the youngsters decided to play a game of cricket. Anyone whose surname was Chafékar, or who lived inside the compound wall, would be on one team while the rest would join the other. Heads were counted and when the Chafékar team was short by four, Baba was sent to the servants' quarters to round up the young boys who lived there, and who were often called upon to make up a quorum. While he was waiting by the Watson cottage, shouting for a fourth to come forward, a head popped up from behind the bushes and the Watson boy offered to make up the team. Baba had scarcely said yes when Christopher scrambled over the hedge. He gave his scraped knee a quick rub and ran after the boys, who were impatient to begin play. Christopher and Baba were the opening batsmen that afternoon, and their friendship was sealed when they scored a century in a partnership that was accommodating, instinctive and bold.

From that day forward, Christopher, who was older than Baba by one year, would visit him after school, after Mrs. Watson had retired to her bedroom, her shutters closed against the steamy glare and the persistent *cooke-cooke-cooke* of the woodpecker that refused to be dislodged from the ashoka tree outside her window. "Whoever coined afternoon siestas, Mother says, was a genius. Without them she would never have survived this ghastly heat."

Christopher was a garrulous boy who spoke only a hand-ful of Marathi words, and because he chattered on in English, he unwittingly forced Baba to become a better listener. Although he was acquiring a good grounding in grammar at the Christian Mission School, Baba lacked fluency in the spoken word. Consequently, he paid close attention when Christopher talked about his family, and forced himself to use new words when imparting information concerning his own. He found himself talking mostly about his father, and how he excelled at everything he undertook: business, tennis, horse riding, even standing on his head. Baba could tell that Christopher was curious about his and Nanasahib's relationship, listening with envy whenever Baba described the way they would race each other at the turf club, or take part in the doubles tennis tournaments at the Gym.

As the months went by the two boys became inseparable, and many a time Baba was forced to ignore his brothers when they teased him and Christopher in Marathi about their growing friendship. Although the four Chafékar siblings were born within a short span of five years, the older three often ganged up and taunted Baba for being a baby who insisted on getting his way. Now they started to call Christopher "Topher, the Red-Faced." Baba did his best to ignore them, and when they were away from Chafékar Wadi he and Christopher would dash to the canal and drag their heels along the sometimes shallow, drought-stricken waterbed, or climb trees to establish who had the least fear of heights. They would destroy anthills with bare feet while giving wide berth to a tall teak under which had been spotted a poison-ous, speckled snake. They used the tennis net like a hurdle and played badminton when the air was still; and in March, they fashioned kites from transparent, colourful paper, and when afternoon breezes picked up, raced them against each other under a blue-bowl sky. Baba tried to get Christopher to become a member of the turf club but Christopher refused, having taken a bad tumble off a horse when he was very young.

Because his father had been the Secretary of Gordon Square, Christopher knew the clubhouse—now Chafékar Wadi—like the back of his hand and often confounded Baba by remaining hidden for several minutes at a time. And when the servants scolded them for getting underfoot, they would escape to the outer cottages, one of which was now a guest-house. One day, on the ground floor of this guesthouse, in the back room that used to be a granary, they stumbled upon a seated man, his forehead most improbably making contact with the floor.

Baba was fascinated by this physical feat. "How can you do that?' he said.

The man lifted his head. "This is my permanent position."

Baba was horrified. "Were you born like this?"

The man laughed bitterly. "No, son. Once I was like you, running and playing with my friends. But it was my fate that I end up like this in my old age."

Baba recognized the woman who did the gardening as she walked into the guesthouse through the back door. "I told at the big house that my father would be here for the day," she said, an audible click at the back of her throat.

"That's all right," Baba said. "He can rest here for as long as he wants."

The upside-down man was scrutinizing Baba's face and now he declared: "Everything will go tolerably well during the next ten years. But in your twenty-fifth year there will be great change accompanied by enormous turbulence and turmoil. I see no illness for you, no death. Just turbulence and turmoil."

"Let's go, Vijay." Christopher's voice was urgent as he tugged on Baba's shirt.

The hair on the back of his neck tingling, Baba, along with Christopher, who had become the colour of bone, walked backwards from the room, and as soon as they were outside, they sprinted from the cottage towards the cricket field where they could breathe again and blot out the sad plight of the contorted man. Baba did not translate for Christopher what the man had prophesied, but from that day forward the boys avoided entering the guesthouse, instead preferring to spend time in the second cottage that contained long polished tables and books that had once belonged to the club's library and had been given away along with the property when it changed hands.

This was, without doubt, their most favourite place to be. Here, amidst the distinctive smell of scholarship and leather, life acquired for them a pleasurable focus. They would move about quietly, as though in a picture gallery, standing in front of one shelf and then another, reaching up on tiptoe in order to read titles on the higher shelves. And when they were done perusing, they would each pluck a book, settle themselves in a winged armchair, and become lost even to each other.

Baba was now doing Shakespeare in school but his favourite books were detective novels and he read and reread Agatha Christie, Arthur Conan Doyle and G.K. Chesterton, cheering on the sleuths as they hunted and identified the perpetrators who then became subject to the impartial measures of Law.

But much as he tried, Baba could not forget the deformed figure he and Christopher had stumbled upon in the guest-house. He asked his mother, without mentioning the prophecy, whether she had ever met the strangely misshapen man.

His mother answered right away. "Yes. Your father even offered to pay for his treatment but he's too scared to go under the knife. He pretends to know how to read faces but I understand that nothing he predicts ever comes true."

~

Vasanti had become quietly fearful during the contorted man's prophecy, for Baba was now in his twenty-fifth year, and was greatly relieved to hear Ramabai's assertion that the so-called visionary was in truth an imposter. Nevertheless, she slid down in bed and, swallowing the lump in her throat, told Baba she was sleepy and faced the wall.

There had been stretches in Vasanti's childhood when she had felt isolated—although never unloved or uncared for—and now, after all those lonesome years, she could scarcely believe her luck that her husband of a few weeks had not only become her tutor, but was also treating her as a friend by telling her childhood stories about his English companion. She imagined Christopher to be a lanky boy with freckled skin made ruddier by repeated exposure to the sun, flexing wild eyebrows that collided in a bridge above his nose. Baba would have been a gangly teenager, quiet (for she had yet to see him in conversation with his brothers), doing his homework with the same intensity with which he was now urging her to memorize two-letter words. Gazing at the life-size portrait of Ramabai in the drawing room (Vasanti had yet to see a lovelier face) she envisioned Baba's curly hair flattened by a cricket cap, demonstrating to his mother his improved bowling.

The one remaining mystery was Nanasahib. Much as she tried to visualize youngest son and father in each other's company, she couldn't. One night she asked Baba whether they still went riding together or paired up for tennis tournaments.

Without lowering his newspaper, Baba said, "Not since he shifted permanently to Pegasus many years ago."

"But he comes here every now and then, does he not?" Vasanti asked. "I'm sure if you asked him to go riding with you or to play tennis, he would."

Baba was silent.

"Or perhaps you could go to the stud farm."

With an irritated click of his tongue, Baba lowered his newspaper and said in a voice that was cold and unsparing, "I will ask for your suggestions concerning Nanasahib, Vasanti, when I need them. Until then, keep your ideas about my tennis and my riding to yourself."

Eyes filling rapidly, Vasanti stumbled to the bathroom and remained there until he had turned off the light.

The following morning Baba seemed his usual self; and his mood and tone were unperturbed as he told her that their evening lesson would have to be cancelled. "I will be late coming home and you are not to wait up for me," he added, setting down his cup of tea.

Vasanti, still shaken by his puzzling and aggressive response to the topic of horses and tennis and Nanasahib, now wondered with a sinking heart whether he was punishing her for the uninvited suggestions of the previous night. But not wishing to question him and upset him further, she kept her disappointment to herself.

The next night he was once again delayed and she was lying in bed counting the pendulum swings as the clock struck its midnight hour, when he opened the door and walked silently into the dressing room; she had left on his bedside lamp. A few minutes later he got into bed, and when she did not hear the expected rustle of his newspaper, she turned around, thinking he must have fallen asleep. Not only was he awake, but he was looking at her.

"Didn't you get my message not to wait up for me?"

"Yes. But the servant said you'd be back by eleven!" She pointed to the newspaper. "You can read. I won't disturb you."

"Can't you follow simple instructions, Vasanti?"

She blinked back her tears.

"It's just that I don't want you to take for granted that I will teach you English every single evening or that I will be home for dinner every night."

When she did not respond, he continued, "In fact I've been thinking it's high time I got you a tutor."

"But why?" A slight tremor passed through her chin.

"Because I'm very busy at work and you are getting too dependent on me. Sheela told me that when you went for the ladies' picnic to the orange groves, all you could think about was getting back in time for your lesson."

"It was too hot even in the shade," Vasanti grumbled. "And we'd been there since eleven in the morning."

"I don't want you to think about your lessons all the time, Vasanti. Is that clear?"

She nodded.

He picked up the newspaper.

She tried to settle for the night, but after tossing and turning for a little while she said, "You won't get me a tutor, will you?"

"I will if you don't go to sleep."

"You know I can't sleep when the light is on."

"The logical thing would have been to turn it off, don't you think?"

"Maybe next time I will. But then you won't be able to read."

"I can always read in the sitting room downstairs."

He switched off the lamp. But she thought she detected a note of humour in his voice.

As soon as Baba walked into the bedroom the following week, Vasanti, who had been waiting for him, got off the sofa and said, "A parcel was delivered this afternoon. I left it next to your desk."

He shrugged out of his shoes. "Must be the English primers I ordered."

"They are here already?"

It had been a long day at the courts and he stood there rubbing the back of his neck.

Vasanti said, "I've laid your fresh clothes and towel in the bathroom. And earlier today I made you the coconut karanji you like. I'll ask the servant to bring it up now."

"You may open the parcel," he said, shrugging out of his coat.

Later, after he had eaten, she passed him the primers and seemed startled when their fingers made contact, for she turned her face away, blushing.

He appeared not to notice and continued to sift through the books. "I hope they are the right ones. If Christopher's mother were alive, she would have guided me."

"I hope I can meet Christopher someday. I haven't seen his father yet."

"If you are that keen, I will introduce you."

She must have recognized his teasing tone, for she ignored the offer.

"When did Christopher leave for England?"

"About six years ago."

"And you haven't seen him since?"

"He returned thrice, the last time after his mother passed away. Just before the war began."

"Why did he leave?"

"To study Engineering. Vasanti, all these questions are keeping us from your lesson."

"Forget about the lesson."

He pretended to be shocked.

"Tell me about Christopher instead."

A new school year had begun. By now Mrs. Watson was aware of Baba and Christopher's friendship. The first time Christopher introduced him, she remarked, "Without the darkening of the skin brought on by the sun, you most certainly could be taken for a European. What with your height, those grey eyes and brown hair . . ." She made it sound like a compliment. She was short herself, narrow of hips and shoulders, and spoke in a sighing way as though Life in the Colonies was preternaturally burdensome and she was never quite sure whether she was meeting its challenge. She dabbed a rolled handkerchief continuously on her face and trailed a scent of eau de cologne wherever she went.

One day, when Christopher and Baba were drinking lemonade underneath the awning of the Watson veranda, Mrs. Watson, who had just returned from supervising the flushing-out and killing of a large rat in her vegetable patch, told them that if they wished to continue their friendship, it was imperative that Mr. Watson never learn of it. Quite struck by the apparent contradiction in her attitude towards their camaraderie versus that of her husband, the boys looked at each other but said nothing. She held out a book to Baba. It was *The Wind in the Willows* by Kenneth Grahame. The gift was accompanied by sage advice that he would remember from time to time: "If you wish to read, write and speak proper English, Vijay, treat Patience not as Virtue but as Staunch Necessity."

The monsoons swept into the region early that year. As a thick curtain of water blocked air from filtering in through the open windows, Baba and Christopher did their homework seated across from each other at the long table in the library. When they were hungry, Ramabai sent tall glasses of buttermilk and bowls of sugared almonds to feed their brains.

One day, struggling with a lengthy essay he was attempting to write, Baba complained bitterly that he was not getting anywhere. Christopher pulled a dustsheet off an adjacent chair and offered to assist.

"Why are you so eager to help me?" Baba said.

"Because you're my best friend," was the simple reply.

"What about your school friends?"

"None like you." Christopher took off his newly acquired glasses and polished them against the cotton of his trousers.

"My mother thinks you must have been an Indian in your past life because you feel so comfortable with us," Baba said.

"What do *you* think?"

"I think she's right."

~

Baba was becoming familiar with the attentiveness that would cross Vasanti's face whenever she was listening to one of his childhood tales. And looking at her, he thought how unrealistic his initial resolution to ignore her had been. She was far away from her maiden home and even though Sheela had told him that she was taking good care of her, civility and friendship was the least he could offer his new wife. He knew she liked him, and he found beguiling the transparence that her innocence bred, for she was unabashedly open with him and did not think there was any need to be otherwise.

Just the previous night, he had walked into the dressing room to see her struggle to remove the clasp of her chain, and when he stood there watching, she'd looked at him in exasperation and said, "Aren't you going to help me?"

He moved forward, and after she swept the bun that was covering her nape out of his way, he undid the clasp, his fingers brushing her neck. Her cheeks reddening, she had taken the chain from his hand and hurried into the bathroom, forgetting to leave it behind on the dressing table as she was normally accustomed to do.

Vasanti now said, "I think Christopher's mother did not want his father to know about your friendship because she knew he would not like it if his son was mixing with us."

"That's a ridiculous thing to say. If that were the case, why does Mr. Watson continue to live here all alone, inside our compound, when he could if he wished rent a cottage alongside English families elsewhere? No, he's an odd man by half and has always been that way."

"Maybe."

Baba could tell by Vasanti's tone that she was not convinced. She switched off her lamp and, like always, curled away from him and faced the wall. And now that he had touched her neck and breathed in the mogra scent of her hair, he found cumbersome his resolve to limit their relationship to a simple camaraderie. Nonetheless, he reminded himself that it was nearing the middle of March, and that he was going away soon. It would be wrong of him therefore to take advantage of her, particularly when she had no idea that he was leaving.

Even so, he found himself saying, "Vasanti, how is it that you don't need much space to sleep?"

She turned around. "Because in Poona I always slept, between my aunts. I had to teach myself to sleep without moving."

"You didn't have a bed of your own?"

"I did. Appa got me a cot when I grew older, but because I had always slept between them, I found the cot too lonely."

After a moment or two she said, "I suppose you never slept between your parents?"

"No."

"Your brothers?"

"Not even in the same room."

"How come?"

"I don't know. They've always been very different from me. They don't like riding or reading or playing tennis. And I wouldn't be surprised if they still breathe and dream about making Surya Spinning Cotton Mills bigger and better."

"Can I ask you something?" She searched his face before continuing. "Why are you so silent during mealtimes? Surely you can partake in some of their conversation, some of the time?"

"Not really," he said. "I'm not acquainted or interested in their day-to-day dealings, and since business is all they ever talk about, I have nothing to say." There was yet another perfectly good reason why he avoided their company, but it was a justification that he had no desire to share.

Before Vasanti could ask him any more questions, Baba said, "You are always asking me about myself. Why don't you ever tell me anything about your family?"

"What would you like to know?"

"Tell me about your father."

She looked down. "If I talk about him, it'll only make me miss him more. But do you remember meeting my uncle Vishnupant at our wedding?" She had never uttered the words *our wedding* before, and he could see that something about them caused her to smile.

"I do," Baba said, not understanding the flicker of delight.

"Because he is a professor, people think that Vishnupant is stern and strict and very orthodox. But in reality he is nothing like that. He condemns caste segregation and thinks that entry into temples for Untouchables should be made into law. He believes in widow remarriage and thinks women should go to college."

"Do you agree with him?"

"Most certainly I do."

Baba was amused by the way she idealized her uncle.

Remembering her interest in history, he quizzed her about the Maratha Kingdom (without knowing anything about it himself) and much to his delight she was able to quote facts and figures and relate the detailed biography of its venerated leader Shivaji Maharaj.

Later, as Baba switched off the lamp, the thought occurred to him that at some fundamental level he and Vasanti understood each other. The notion was comforting.

~ EIGHT ~

SOON IT WAS NEARING the time to lay final plans for Baba's journey to England. Consequently, he met up with Nanasahib's travel secretary, and after giving the man instructions, decided to return home early.

He asked the servant to bring up some tea, then climbed the stairs to Vasanti. She was nowhere to be seen. He stepped into the terrace and saw her right away, walking all by herself alongside the canal. He cupped his mouth and shouted for her to come in. She didn't look up. He called out again. This time she raised her eyes, but only to track five birds winging their way across the jungle. The servant entered the terrace and Baba pointed at Vasanti and told him to fetch Memsahib right away. He stood watching even as the boy ran down the back stairs, opened the gate and approached

Vasanti. She turned around and waved to him. The boy said something and now she followed him quickly up the stone steps and across the lawn, and when she entered the bedroom panting, Baba was standing just inside the terrace door.

"What's wrong?" she said; there was panic in her voice.

"What were you doing down there?"

"When I was walking the grounds I saw deer on the other side of the water. I wished to take a closer look, that's all."

"Deer?" He strode forward and stood opposite her by the foot of the bed.

"Yes."

"Do you not know that earlier this year, less than a furlong along the water's edge, a tiger killed a deer that was drinking there?"

She was indignant. "No one told me."

He encircled her wrist with his fingers. "Promise me you will not go down to the canal. Especially not at this time of evening, and never alone."

"Had I known about the deer kill, do you think I would have gone?"

He tightened his grip. "Promise me!"

"I promise!"

He saw that his forbidding intensity had brought tears to her eyes. He let go, wishing instead that he could take her into his arms.

She brought up her wrist and rubbed it.

"I'm having tea. Would you like a cup?"

"I'm not thirsty," she said, "and I need to wash my hands."

Wishing he could have reacted less harshly, he went into the terrace, shaken by dread at what might have happened if indeed there had been a tiger lurking. He poured out a cup of tea and stood there, watching it turn cold.

Even though Nagpur was several hundred miles distant from Poona, Vasanti did not miss her maiden home too much, for her aunts were prolific correspondents and a communication would arrive from them like clockwork on either a Thursday or Friday afternoon. They took turns writing to her, and a single side of the government-issued mustard postcard was sufficient space in which to convey their news. Vasanti's replies to them were sometimes lengthy, other times brief, depending on whether anything newsworthy had occurred at Chafékar Wadi during the previous week.

They had met her early announcement—filled with exclamation marks—regarding Baba's tutoring with delighted shock. They wrote back immediately and recommended that since Baba was showering on her this kind of attention, she in turn should study hard and prove just what a good student she could be. Somewhat annoyed that they would question her diligence, she nevertheless forgave them and began adding in English *I miss you* (words she had requested Baba to translate for her) as a last message in every letter before signing off.

After a month had passed in her new home and many detailed letters had been sent to Poona, her aunts wrote that they were very pleased by the way Vasanti had blended in with her new family. However, they had one minor quibble: They wanted her to write more about her interactions with Baba when he was not teaching her English. Was he gentle, understanding, kind? She replied that their exchanges were more or less limited to the hour spent together during her lessons, barring the time he told her stories about his friend Christopher; but then she had already informed them about that.

In the next letter, the aunts remembered how Vasanti's mother had passed away on the eighth of April in 1926 and every year on that date Sitarampant would perform a religious ceremony in her memory. The aunts wrote that this year Vasanti and her father's absence would be sorely felt; they suggested that it would be a good thing if Vasanti observed on that anniversary day a simple fast.

When Vasanti told Sheela that she was planning a twenty-four-hour fast, one without eating or imbibing a drop of water, Sheela was quick to dissuade her. The heat wave had begun early in March and cricket practices and matches had been cancelled for weeks. It was an exceptionally hot

April as well, with temperatures soaring to 46 degrees Celsius and many at Chafékar Wadi were complaining of severe headaches accompanied by high fever and heat exhaustion. The gardeners had been instructed to stay indoors during the hours around noon, and were told to keep to the shade as much as possible. The newspaper delivery boy complained that his hands were blistered from clutching the metal handlebars of his bicycle; Amita bandaged the boy's hands so they would not become further chafed.

Sheela said, "I know this fast you wish to perform is in memory of your dear mother, so I will not ask you to break it by partaking of food. But I must insist that you consume water, fruit juice, milk and buttermilk throughout the day."

Vasanti had no choice but to agree.

The uncovered south-facing terrace was a sun-trap and on the night of her fast Vasanti lay on her bed, cold wet cloth pressed to her forehead and throat. Baba had come home early that day, complaining of sore eyes, and when Sheela informed him of Vasanti's fast, he had not been pleased.

She now asked Baba, who was tossing and turning in the dark, whether his eyes were still watering.

"How do you feel, Vasanti, is more the question."

"I'm fine," she said. "Glasses of buttermilk, milk, fruit juice, lots of water: I don't think I should even call it a fast."

"Do you keep one every year?"

"I do. Until last year it was for my mother; this year it

will be for my father as well." Her voice was matter-of-fact.

"I wish you could have met my mother," Baba said. "She was only forty-two when she died."

So taken aback was Vasanti by his reference to Ramabai, that she asked him in a small and faltering voice, "Was she ailing for a long time?"

Baba said he thought she might have been and that he still regretted not reporting her fragile health to the doctor the very day he had come home from school and noticed her sitting on the sofa, clearly unwell. He turned to face Vasanti and told her the full story.

"Can I fetch you a shawl?" Baba had asked his mother.

And while he was wrapping it around Ramabai's shoulders, she patted the seat next to her. "Come and sit down."

He sprawled across the sofa and placed his feet on his mother's lap.

"In a few months you will be facing your matriculation exams," she said. "It's high time, don't you think, that we discussed the prospect of you working alongside your brothers after you have graduated?"

He was silent.

"All three were complaining to me only yesterday that you show no interest in attending the Mills."

"But I'm only in my last year of school."

"Your brothers started going to the Mills in their final year, did they not?"

He decided right there to take the plunge. "What would you say, Aai, if I said I don't want to make my name as a textile manufacturer? That I want to become a lawyer instead?"

"A lawyer?"

"Yes."

She smiled. "Have I not seen you show interest in my brother's legal cases all these years? How old were you the first time you attended court with Bhiku?"

"Eleven."

"Have you spoken to your father about this?"

"Can you?" he said. He had never before asked her to speak on his behalf.

"If I have seen and noted your interest in the justice system, will he not have too? He returns from Bombay tomorrow."

"But what if he gets angry and forbids me from doing what I want? What if he talks me into doing something I don't want to do by giving all kinds of reasons while claiming that his advice is for my own good?"

"There is a chance that he may do all of that, but what alternative do you have? You can't study law without his permission, can you?"

"It's so easy talking to you, Aai!"

His mother gave a satisfied smile. "I wasn't always so compliant and understanding, you know. But where it comes to you children, it's important that I understand your needs." She rewrapped the shawl around her shoulders. "Talk to your father and see what he has to say. Your brothers complain that you have him twisted around your finger—the only one in the family who has."

"That's not true. You have him twisted too. He's always praising your wisdom and telling us that we must obey you, no matter what."

She let out an uncharacteristic splutter, whether one of derision or approval he could not tell.

Baba decided he would speak to his father on a Tuesday, the one day his father was away from the Mills and working in his less busy office in the business district of the city. And so Baba climbed the high stone steps and knocked on Nanasahib's office door, the sound made inaudible by the jack-hammering from the dug-out street below. When there was no reply, he opened the door and entered Nanasahib's room. His father was startled to see him.

"Never do that," he said. "Never come here unannounced. I could have been in an important meeting."

Baba stepped back.

Nanasahib pushed forward in his chair. "What is it? Is your mother all right?"

"She's fine."

He waved for Baba to sit on the neatly made-up cot in the corner, and rubbing the back of his neck, said, "You aren't in any trouble, are you?"

Baba shook his head.

Nanasahib reached for the accounts ledger that was open on his desk. "I want you to take a look at this. The profits this year are not as good as I expected them to be."

Baba examined the credit column; it appeared quite healthy to him.

"I came across some Japanese samples of fabric the other day. Judging by their quality, I don't think it'll be long before Japan enters the export market. If that happens, it will provide India with competition that does not exist today, at least not to any great extent."

Baba handed back the ledger.

"Your brothers think it is time to diversify—not just stick to the cotton trade. What do you think?"

Baba hesitated.

"Come on, you must have some opinion on the matter."

"That's just it," Baba burst out. "I don't have the brains for this kind of business."

Nanasahib narrowed his eyes. "Then what in your view *do* you have the brains for?"

"Law. I would like to ask your permission to study law."

Nanasahib looked down at the ledger and riffled its pages. "What does your mother say?"

Baba was silent.

"I know you always discuss things with her before coming to me."

"She didn't say no."

"She didn't say yes?"

"She never says yes before you say yes."

"I'll have you know I learned diplomacy from your mother."

But Baba had learned something from Ramabai too: the power of silence. He continued to sit there, looking down at his lap.

At last, Nanasahib said, "Where would you study law?"

"I've been talking to Christopher. He says I could fill terms in London and be admitted to the Inner Temple in due course."

Nanasahib contemplated a stray bee on the window ledge, fluttering its wings in an attempt to fly. Looking at Baba, he said, "Since your heart seems to be set on it, study law. But I don't want you going away. Study it here, in Nagpur."

Grateful and elated that Nanasahib had acceded so easily to his wish, Baba didn't argue. He knew he could travel to London later, after obtaining his initial degree. He reached down to touch his father's feet, but Nanasahib would have none of it: he clasped his youngest to his chest. There was a lump the size of a large pearl in Baba's throat when he bounded down the staircase, and hurried out into the noise.

~

"When did you first know you wanted to study law?" Vasanti asked Baba.

Baba yawned. "I can't say I remember an absolute first time. It feels as though I've always been interested in it." He turned in bed and told her it was time they got some sleep.

But Vasanti stayed awake, thinking of Baba's story and wishing she could remember her mother. She had one photograph of her, speckled with age, a far shot where she was standing in front of a door, her eyes squinting into the distance. By contrast, the Chafékar family albums were thick. There were photographs of a boyish and razor-thin Raosahib dressed in a European suit and wearing a hat, standing next to the Mills when they were a mere cluster of tin-roof sheds, and several other albums of family functions, ending with the photographs taken at Vasanti and Baba's wedding.

Sheela had driven her past the now-modernized Mills, and past the Old Secretariat and the High Court. Once when they were driving to the Gymkhana for some ladies' lunch, Vasanti had told Sheela that the biggest change that had occurred in her life during the previous year after the loss of her father was in her perception of what a husband was or could be.

When Vasanti was around nine years old, a young woman living in a small stone house down the lane had committed suicide by hanging herself from the rafters. Even though the details of the tragedy were never discussed within Vasanti's earshot, she nonetheless had the impression that the wretched girl's husband had driven her to this calamitous act. Vasanti knew the man by sight. He was employed in a foundry near the railway station, and would pass their house every morning and evening, before and after work. He was a familiar figure in the neighbourhood, and consequent to the tragedy, Vasanti, drawn against her will towards the macabre, began to watch him, peeping from behind the curtain of her window to see whether she could detect in his face or deportment any indication of his murderous state. She observed him for weeks, and apart from the fact that the calves and ankles underneath his dhotar were spindly and covered in blue blotches, and his thick ears stuck out of his narrow clean-shaven head in a grotesque way, there was no outward sign at all of his mean and treacherous heart.

One day, at the time he normally returned from work, she stood at their gate and stared at him openly, and when he came abreast he bared a crooked grin that showed missing teeth. Leering at her, he said, "What are you looking at?"

She dropped her gaze and remained rooted to her place until he had entered his house. Thereafter, her nights were filled with brassy dreams, and her days in conceiving ways in which she would never again have to lay eyes on him. Over time the memory receded to the back of her mind but whenever she heard the word *husband*, a chilly hand would grip her heart. And when her aunts had told her she was getting married, the old memories of the errant man had surfaced once again.

"It wasn't until a fortnight into my marriage," she told Sheela, "that I realized that not only is my husband not going to drive me to suicide, but that he is incapable of hurting me or anyone else."

Sheela concurred and pressed her hand and told her she had nothing to worry about.

~ NINE ~

AT THE BEGINNING OF APRIL, a letter arrived
from England. Christopher, who had written but
twice since the start of the war, had finally found
time to respond to Baba's correspondence. During the previous five months, Baba had sent his friend three letters to
say that he would be arriving in London sometime in
August. There had been no reply. Now, to Baba's chagrin,
Christopher's letter was brief, and made no reference to
Baba's plans for travel to England or to his request about
whether he could stay with his friend until suitable accommodation could be found.

Instead, Christopher apologized for not keeping in
touch, then went on to express disappointment that his
poor eyesight had rendered him ineligible to enlist for

front-line combat. In London there were shortages of food, of fuel, of clothes. Nonetheless he was grateful that for the moment, at least, the bombing had stopped. He ended the letter by referring to the conversation that he and Baba had had before the war, regarding the possibility of Baba travelling to London to fulfill his bar terms. He wrote now that Baba should postpone his coming over indefinitely, until such time that Europe was liberated and normalcy restored.

Baba's heart fluttered uneasily. Of course it was ill-advised to travel under such fraught conditions. But Christopher did not know the specifics of what had happened to trigger Baba's decision to leave Nagpur at this particular time. It was not information he wished to convey to Christopher, or indeed disclose to Vasanti, because it would mean admitting that the unmentionable reason had everything to do with his father. And it had everything to do with his father. Much as scholarship at the Inner Temple was something Baba had set his heart upon a long time ago, he would have postponed his dream if only Nanasahib had proffered an olive branch, or made certain pledges. But, there was continued silence from Pegasus and an unwillingness on his father's part to meet Baba's terms.

Consequently, it was as important as it had been five months ago for Baba to seek distance.

~

A couple of days later, Baba went to the Mills to meet Nanasahib's travel secretary. The man informed him that he had managed to book passage on a ship sailing from Bombay to Liverpool on the third of July.

Baba was annoyed. "Didn't I say that I wished to leave towards the middle of July?"

"Yes, Sahib," Mr. Pandey replied. "But there is no ship leaving for England later in the month. And obtaining even this secured berth would have been impossible but for the monetary inducement that had to be arranged."

"So there's no way we can change my sailing date?"

"That's right, Sahib. Also, I've made an appointment for you with the port and passport authorities. Here, I've written down the details."

Baba took the scrap of paper from Mr. Pandey's hand and inserted it into his shirt pocket. He cancelled his riding appointment and arrived home early, all the while struggling to think of an easy way to break to Vasanti the news of his London plans—now so fast approaching.

She was fast asleep on the sofa in their bedroom, a turned-down magazine on her stomach, one arm covering her eyes, the fingers of the other trailing the floor. In sleep she looked even younger, perhaps fifteen, and even though the curtains were drawn, the hot afternoon had imparted to her skin a rosy sheen. The bottom of her sari had travelled up her legs, exposing soles and calves that were startlingly fair, and her long plait had slipped out of its bun and lay awkwardly coiled behind her head. He gently eased the plait away from her neck and laid it alongside her body, and even as he was moving away, she half opened her eyes, mumbled something in a dreamy voice, then lapsed back into sleep.

Baba checked his watch. It was almost time for the late-afternoon broadcast. He went downstairs to the drawing room and turned on the radio. The announcer talked about the discussions that were underway between Whitehall in London and the Indian National Congress in Delhi regarding the conflict in Europe. The British government had sent Mr. Stafford Cripps to negotiate with the Indian National Congress a deal that would persuade the subcontinent to give its total cooperation to the Allied cause during the war. However, the Congress Party was not amenable to considering the request, and was threatening to withdraw its support unless India was guaranteed immediate self-rule. Baba did not understand Congress's intransigence, particularly because the party leaders knew full well that Mr. Cripps did not have the authority or the will to grant autonomy. Besides, the immediate withdrawal of British power was nothing short of foolhardy, for where was the legitimate body to replace it? And without a ruling government, society and indeed the nation was bound to dissolve into lawlessness, even chaos. And though he wanted independence, Baba deplored the fact that Gandhi in his perverse way seemed unfazed by the prospect of anarchy. Frustrated by the sense-less politicking, he switched off the radio and went upstairs.

Vasanti was no longer on the sofa. Baba was sitting at his desk when she came out of the dressing room, her face washed and scrubbed, her eyes heavy with sleep. She was surprised to see him.

"Our lessons have been losing steam lately," Baba said. "So I thought I'd come home early today."

She took her seat beside him and stifled a yawn.

"Are you fully awake, Vasanti? We have just over two months in which to learn the basic rules. After that you will have to teach yourself."

"I don't understand."

"I need you to work harder because . . . I'm going away."

She searched his face.

"I'm going to study law, in London."

"But you already have a law degree."

"From Nagpur University, I do."

"So then why must you go?"

"I want to be called to the bar. I wish to become a barrister."

"But there's fighting in England." Her voice was incred-ulous, and her expression told him that she didn't believe what she was hearing.

"In Europe. No Axis powers have landed in England." He hoped she had not seen the pictures of the Blitz.

"This is all so sudden." Her voice faltered and the notebook slipped from her lap to the floor.

He retrieved it for her, overcome by guilt. "The truth, Vasanti, is that I've been planning on studying abroad for quite some time now."

"Then why did you not tell me before?" He could see she was hurt and trying not to show it. "Does the rest of the family know?"

"Yes."

"My sisters-in-law?"

He nodded, surprised that none of them had spilled the beans. The previous November, soon after they had learned of his plans to leave for London, they had pestered him continuously, even begged him to defer his decision to travel abroad. He had been as adamant then as now. Perhaps, he surmised, they had been hoping that he would find it difficult to leave Vasanti and therefore had decided not to mention anything to her.

"It's no secret," he said, "that I've always wanted to be called to the bar. Even my mother knew that." He kept his tone matter-of-fact.

The stricken look on her face told him that she was humiliated that he had not told *her*.

"How long will we be gone?" she said.

"What do you mean, *we?*"

"Well, aren't you going to take me with you?"

"No. I don't think that will be possible."

"I thought that since we're married . . ."

"I'll be gone for a year, most likely two, and it will be very difficult for you to leave India for that long."

"As many as that?" She touched her fingers to the bottom of her throat, then covered her face with her hands, too embarrassed to let him see her tears.

"Vasanti." He reached forward and gently held her wrist.

She extricated herself, ran into the bathroom, and closed the door.

He followed her there and knocked. "Vasanti?"

She didn't answer.

"I should have told you before. But time passes quickly, and before you know it, I'll be back."

When she didn't reply, he moved away and slumped into his chair. While waiting for her to reappear, he tried to read the newspaper.

When next he glanced at the dressing room, Vasanti was watching him from the doorway, her eyes watery and red.

He got up and pulled back a chair for her, and said, "Come and sit down."

Perhaps responding to the unexpected gentleness in his voice, she moved forward slowly.

He had earlier written the letters *a*, *b*, *c*, *d*, *e* across the top of the page and asked now that she reproduce them.

And as she began to write, he stood behind her. After a moment or two he placed his hand on top of hers, and guided her pen to demonstrate how the letters ought to be shaped. Vasanti shifted in her chair and leaned farther over her notebook, and, enchanted by the closeness of her, Baba resisted for a brief while the sensible voice in his head that was telling him to stop breathing in her scent. And when he stepped back he was surprised by the speed with which his heart was beating.

The day following the disclosure of Baba's news, Vasanti said, "Do none of the family mind that you are leaving?"

"Why do you ask?"

"I thought they might have tried to dissuade you. England is so far away. And there is the fighting."

"If the Axis powers had landed in Great Britain I would have postponed my plans. So I'm not worried about my safety, and I don't want you to be either."

"This morning I asked my sisters-in-law what they think about you leaving. All they said was, once you make up your mind there is very little anyone can do to change it."

"I'm afraid they know me too well. What else did they say?"

"Sheelatai said she extracted a promise that you will not eat meat, or drink spirits."

"Yes, and I intend to keep that promise."

And just like that, as he was looking at her, the tears rolled down her cheeks.

She dabbed her handkerchief to her eyes and after giving one last shudder, said, "I understand from them that you made plans to go away even before we were married. So why did you not say anything? There must have been a reason for you not to tell me."

"During all those stories about Christopher and my mother . . . I wish now I had told you then."

Her nose red and glistening, she waited for him to continue.

"It's just that you are so very young, Vasanti, and so very innocent. I was afraid if I told you, you would get worried and become sad, just the way you are now. I wanted you to feel settled at Chafékar Wadi first, before springing the news. Besides, I didn't know for certain whether I had a berth on that ship or not. And as soon as I knew I had, you were the very first person I told."

She raised the handkerchief once again and this time covered her face with it.

The required paperwork took him a week to complete, and when it was done Baba right away informed Vasanti that his travel plans were now truly set. She placed her fingers at the bottom of her throat and Baba felt relieved that this time there were no tears. She had been morose and cheerless the first forty-eight hours after hearing the news, yet as the days passed she seemed to have grown used to the idea of him leaving and had thrown herself into her lessons with renewed determination and zeal.

Watching Vasanti at work over her notebook now, Baba felt that he had failed her in more ways than one. Not only had he been an ineffective tutor, but he had also visited upon her a grave injustice when, against good judgment, he had agreed to marry before leaving for England. It was unfair of him to have made her a pawn in sealing the bargain with his brothers—something he had done only because he needed their support to study abroad.

Six months ago, when he'd decided to go away, he'd had no idea who Vasanti was or even what she looked like. All he had cared about was that he had made up his mind to leave Chafékar Wadi and nothing was going to stop him. Now he wished he had given his future bride more consideration, for there was little doubt that he would miss her during his London stay. He had only to catch a glimpse of the corners of her mouth, the angle of her shoulders, the set of her jaw to know what kind of mood she was in: cooperative, lazy, playful, sad.

Suddenly consumed by desire, he left the desk and stood at the door of the terrace, gazed blindly at the water undulating in the swimming pool.

After a minute Vasanti came and stood next to him and held out a piece of paper on which was written several times the alphabet, in lower case. He praised her efforts and she looked down, but not before he had seen the pleasure in her eyes. Ever since he had leaned over and guided her writing hand across the page a week ago she had avoided making eye contact, and whenever he was explaining some point of grammar she fixed her gaze not on his face, but on some point beyond. He doubted whether she was aware that the bashful sentiments she bore him were reflected in her face, and he found her sudden shyness captivating because it was so artless and pure.

Early the following morning, he awakened to the noisy sounds of splashing accompanied by the thud of wet clothes being beaten against stone. Mildly irritated that Vasanti was doing her laundry at this unusual hour, he hurried to the bathroom. Its door was not latched properly, and was partially open. The tap was turned on full, the bucket underneath was overflowing and Vasanti was on her haunches, sari ruched up around her waist. Her bare shoulders were bathed golden by a single shaft of the rising sun and the back of her slender neck was covered in fine mist. She finished twisting the underclothes to wring them of excess water and a rounded breast exposed itself when she reached up to put off the tap. He stepped back quietly and walked away.

When she exited the dressing room, he was once again lying in bed. "Why are you up this early?" he asked. "It's not even six o' clock yet."

"We're going to play badminton. My sisters-in-law and I. Before it gets too hot."

"You are?" He was pleasantly surprised. "Whose idea was it?"

"Mine."

"I didn't know you played badminton. But let me not keep you."

He tried to doze off, but when he couldn't, he rang for morning tea and on an impulse removed a pair of binoculars from his wardrobe. His bare feet slipping on the dew, he went to the farther end of the terrace. Raising the glasses to his eyes, he waited a while, but the badminton court remained deserted. He returned to his room, drank tea and then before going in for his bath, thought he would take another look. This time he saw movement on the court. All three of his sisters-in-law were volleying the shuttlecock, and it took him no time to judge that while the others were complete novices, Vasanti's strokes were fluid and strong. And as he stood there watching, he noted with a jealous pang that he had never seen her quite so happy as when she was smashing the shuttlecock, or making drop shots or lobbing it high into the air.

That night he moved restlessly in bed, reminding

himself that now was the time to exert self-control, to abstain, now more than ever because he was soon leaving. But the thought of embarking on his long journey without making that final connection with Vasanti was all of a sudden torturous and unimaginable. He slammed shut his book and, reaching across, touched her shoulder with a gentle hand. She turned around instantly.

Clearing her throat theatrically, she said: "Tiger, tiger . . . something forest something."

He wished he could reward her earnestness with a caress. "Say after me: *Tiger, tiger, burning bright, / In the forests of the night.*"

She repeated the words successfully.

"Do you know what that line means?"

"No."

He translated it for her, then moved to the centre of the bed and took hold of her hand. She searched his face, and whatever it was she saw there made her blush. She snatched back her fingers, sat up in bed and rushed into the dressing room.

And a suspicion that had been lingering inside his head became all at once a certainty: her spinster aunts had failed to inform her about the physical union contained within married life.

～

After a night spent fighting the urge to embrace his wife, Baba knew what he had to do. He sought out Sheela, who was in the garden measuring with her eyes the stems of flowers before snipping them to suit the assortment of vases at her feet. As he helped her fill one with yellow snapdragons, she asked him for the second time to what she owed the pleasure of his company. He told her in as dispassionate a voice as possible that Vasanti had not been explained her conjugal duties. The laughter rose out of Sheela in a merry spurt and she muffled it with the end of her sari. Her body heaving with giggles, she turned from him.

Flummoxed and more than a little annoyed, Baba started to walk away.

"Stop!" Sheela called.

"Only if you stop laughing."

"All right, Baba!"

He glanced around. "Can you not lower your voice?"

She whispered, "Why did you wait so long before coming to me?"

He made as if to leave.

"Stop." Sheela laid down the bunch of flowers she was holding. "It's not that unbelievable, you know, her not knowing anything about—. Her mother died when she was only three and her aunts obviously regarded the subject as unmentionable. Don't look so worried. I'll talk to her."

That night, when Baba came up to bed, Vasanti was

missing. He checked in the terrace: she was crouched in the dark, leaning against the wall, chin resting on steepled knees. Baba held out his hand. She ignored it. He re-entered the room and turned off the light. He had recited in his head the most challenging chapter on Tort Law before she took up her usual position, back turned to him, on her side of the bed. He moved to its middle and laid a hand on her shoulder. To his relief, she did not resist but faced him right away. He pulled her into the crook of his arms. Her loosely plaited hair smelt faintly of crushed flowers and he very tentatively buried his face in its thickness. She trembled but did not pull away.

"It's nothing to be frightened about," he murmured.

Nuzzling into his chest and reaching down, she eased her sari to cover her legs. He was content to be patient that night, and bit by bit the tension left her body; and for the very first time since they were married they fell asleep in each other's arms.

The following night, Baba gathered her to him once again and this time, after holding her for a few minutes, he very slowly hitched up her petticoat underneath the sari and ran his hand up and down her thigh, stopping every now and then when her trembling reached a feverish pitch. Still she did not resist. He brushed his mouth against her cheeks, her forehead, her neck, and when he couldn't take it any slower he rolled her onto her back.

Afterwards, when he was spent and she was turned away, her back pressed into his side, he said, "If I had known it was you that was destined to enter my life, I would have included you in my plans." When she did not respond, he added, "But it's too late to change them now. You do understand that, don't you? My passage is already booked."

"Will you take me with you the next time you go on a long journey?"

"You know I will."

She was silent.

"Look at me."

She turned around. He ran a forefinger around her eyes. "I don't want you to cry."

"I don't want you to go."

"Would you like for me to cancel my plans?" And suddenly, a part of him yearned for her to say, *Yes*.

"No. But I want you to come back soon."

"As soon as I'm called to the bar. I'll not stay a day longer. I promise."

"That's all I'm asking."

As she reached down and pulled up the bedclothes to cover her breasts, she found herself staring at the swishing blades of the fan, and the ardent quiver of bashful happiness flowed through her body long after his had been swallowed by the gentle cadence of sleep.

~ TEN ~

VASANTI COULD NO LONGER FOCUS on her English lessons, and as much as she yearned for Baba to touch her and hold her close, she was anxious every evening when she contemplated the unfamiliar discomfort that lay ahead. Lingering downstairs after dinner, she knitted his sweater, memorized short words, and even stepped out for a walk, only to return because the grounds were not lit and everything appeared ominous and dark. Unlike the time when Baba had told her about his plans for England and she had wept in front of her sisters-in-law, the current cause of her anxiety was private and not one she wished to discuss or share. Yet, she couldn't postpone going upstairs forever. And so the first week passed, and as she became more familiar with Baba she scolded herself for shortening the little time they had together.

One night, when Baba was in a strange mood, turning the pages of his book with unseeing eyes—or so it seemed to her—she said, "The servant came looking for you this afternoon. Said your father wished to see you. Did you meet up with him?" Her voice was tentative for she remembered Baba's livid response the first and only time she had referred to Nanasahib so many weeks ago.

"I did."

"What did he want?"

"He went over the financial details of how and when he will send me money while I am gone."

"He hardly ever comes to Chafékar Wadi these days. I mean, what does he do at the farm? I know he's involved in horse breeding but I thought he had a manager—?"

"What do you mean, what does he do at the farm?" Baba's voice was tight and his eyes bored into her.

"I mean nothing. It was just an idle question."

Vasanti turned away and picked up a magazine, and it was a while before the blurred print assumed legible shape.

Baba had anticipated the day Vasanti's curiosity would be turned in the direction of his father, but was completely unprepared for the nature of her questions. There were many stories he could have told her about Nanasahib: about how close they once were; about how, before he entered middle school, Nanasahib would occasionally ask him to skip classes just so he could spend time with his youngest. It was he who had taught Baba to ride and to play tennis; and whenever he would compare Baba favourably to his younger self, the comparison would cause Baba to smile for days.

And he vividly remembered being broken-hearted when their relationship had first lost its intimacy. It was around the time Baba turned twelve, when Nanasahib purchased the stud farm. All of a sudden Nanasahib's absences from Chafékar Wadi had grown longer; and curiously, whenever Baba asked his father whether he could visit Pegasus there was always some excuse: the farmhouse was being renovated, it was the breeding season, or the dam had collapsed and flooded the fields. Baba felt miffed because the reasons were weak, and he could not understand why Nanasahib did not wish to spend time with him any more.

Once, he'd asked Ramabai why she never visited Pegasus, but his mother had merely shrugged without offering any reply.

Then one day, when he was perhaps thirteen, while resting his head across Ramabai's lap, he held her wrists up to his nose and asked why she never smelt of his father. Nanasahib's rose attar was his signature scent and Baba had often carried his fragrance after a day spent with him. No sooner was the question uttered than he felt his mother's body stiffen, and when he looked into her face he knew he had touched a raw nerve.

"I like roses," he mumbled.

"And I like sandalwood," she said, her tone uncharacteristically cold.

He resolved never to speak of roses again, or of flowers, or for that matter, smells of any kind. And from that time on, even if he wished to describe the mouth-watering aroma of green chilies in the cook's potato preparation, or the heavenly pungent tang of aubergines cooked in oil, he restrained himself. He did not refer to bad smells either: the putrid, mildew odour of the canal in the dry months, the mouth-gagging stench of meat in the markets on the way to school. If smells were a taboo topic for Ramabai, they would be taboo for him, too.

With an annoyed click of his tongue, Baba flipped through the pages of his book and Vasanti realized that bringing up the subject of Nanasahib had once again elicited a strange response. She knew better than to press him for conversation tonight, but no sooner had she started to move away than she felt his hand on her shoulder. He turned her around, sought out her eyes, pulled her to him and covered her mouth with his own.

She had never been kissed before and for the first time experienced an electric feeling that coursed through her body in delightful waves. He was insistent now, as though he couldn't get enough of her, and she entwined her arms around his neck even as his mouth traversed her eyes, her chin, her ears, even her throat.

"My little Vasanti," he murmured, over and over again. "My darling Vasanti love." And a groan of pleasure tinged with sadness escaped her even as she placed an open mouth against his neck and breathed him in.

He urged her to remove her sari. She widened her eyes. Placing a tender hand on her forehead, he said, "Don't be afraid."

Skin hot and bangles tinkling, she undid the six yards, winding them into a bundle around her right arm, and when she was finished he eased the copious cotton from her wrist and dropped it over the side of the bed.

He glanced down and told her to remove her petticoat. "It's all right," he said, his tone gentle.

She untied the drawstring while he unhooked her blouse. After she was divested of them both, she reached down and pulled up the quilt so that it completely covered their bodies. Looking into her eyes, he removed her underclothes, then burrowing under the quilt, he lowered his mouth to her breasts and when she began to moan he moved down, his lips brushing her taut skin as his head travelled lower and lower, and just as he found himself plunging into that salty moist taste of her, she shuddered, and he would have lingered there but for the fact that she was pulling him upwards, taking him by her hands and leading him in.

Afterwards, slipping into her clothes, her senses alive and tingling, she thought: *How ever am I going to live without him?*

Vasanti loved waking early these days, her alarm set for five o'clock. Baba was a light sleeper, turning in bed grumpily if she was too noisy opening the terrace door or too loud in setting down her glass. Tiptoeing into the dressing room, she would quietly gather her clothes, and by the time she was finished bathing he would be sitting on the stool in front of the mirror, waiting his turn to brush his teeth. She would ring for tea and they would drink it together, he unmindful of soggy biscuit quarters falling off and staining his nightshirt and she regarding him rather shyly because he looked so beautiful and strong.

While he was off riding, she would play badminton, and after a late breakfast, wait for him at his desk for yet another of her English lessons, which were now scheduled for the morning. He would leave for the courts after an early lunch, to avoid his brothers, she suspected. The oldest, Suresh, asked Baba every now and again about matters connected to

the legal world, his tone perfunctory, his manner condescending, as though he were wiser than Baba, or cleverer or
harboured some secret knowledge that Baba was much too
young or perhaps ill-equipped to share. Not one of them
referred to his imminent departure and Vasanti knew better
than to seek an explanation for the fissure she saw.

The women of the house spent a lot of time together
and as the weeks passed by, Vasanti's initial liking for Sheela
remained undiminished. Amita spoke her mind a little too
plainly and Vasanti sensed that her youngest sister-in-law
was always watching her.

And sure enough, Amita one day said, "So, you are no
longer a maiden girl, Vasanti, but a full-fledged woman."

Shocked by Amita's sharp discernment, Vasanti dropped
her eyes.

"Amita!" Nina admonished. "They've been married
more than three months now."

"Yet, until a month ago Vasanti looked an innocent
eighteen—"

"Sheelatai," Nina said. "Tell Amita to stop."

But Vasanti, knowing that come July she would in every
way have to fend for herself, met Amita's eyes and said, "You
could say I'm a woman now."

Looking at Baba that night, she felt hurt that he would
want to leave her, especially now, when they were sharing not
only a physical bond but something that went beyond, an

ineffable closeness that was novel and unexpectedly sweet (she couldn't think of a better word). She had been successful in hiding the extreme anxiety and loneliness she felt at the mere thought of his going away, but now her assumed facade was developing cracks and she begged him not to leave.

"I'm going to say this only once: Nothing is going to happen to me. Nothing."

Her left eyelid flickering, she said, "There is something you are not telling me. I can feel it."

"There is nothing to tell."

But even as Baba said this, they both knew he was lying.

Nevertheless, frightened by his pale collapsed mouth and the tightness in his expression, Vasanti relaxed her own, forced a little smile and said, "One, maybe two years from now, you will return and tease me about how upset I was over you leaving, and I will deny any such thing."

The following afternoon, as soon as Vasanti entered the terrace, she knew that something was wrong. Amita's bloodshot eyes were fixed on the jungle beyond the canal, Nina was clutching in her hands a crushed piece of paper and Sheela was pouring tea, the stream of liquid sloshing unevenly inside the cup and spilling onto the saucer.

"What's the matter?" Vasanti whispered into Nina's ear as she slipped into the chair beside her.

Can I? Nina mouthed to Sheela.

"Show it to her," Amita said, her voice shockingly life-less and flat. "For all its reputation, let her see first-hand what kind of a family she is *really* married into."

Nina passed Vasanti the crumpled handwritten sheet, and Vasanti smoothed the creases with her palm and read it:

Amita,

Yogesh should have told you about us before your wedding.
I begged him on several occasions to. But he was afraid to tell his
family because I am not a Brahmin. After you were married
I stopped nagging because the time to say something was past.
Now, I regret to inform you I am carrying his child. Since he
wants nothing to do with me I will go away never to return.
But in order for me to do this I will need for you to make
financial arrangements for his child. I throw myself upon your
mercy. If you wish to communicate with me, send a note with
his driver, who knows all about us.
Yours sincerely,
from one woman to another, both who have been badly duped,
T.L.

Vasanti's first instinct was to avoid looking at Amita, to be spared further sight of the wretchedness and humiliation etched into her face. She reread the note, its sly blend of threats and fact.

Amita said, "Do you remember the euphoria in our family, Sheelatai? Three Gogaté sisters marrying into the Chafékar House! All three must be born lucky to get such a lofty, illustrious match, everyone said." Amita forced the words through her tears.

Sheela jumped up and pulled Amita onto her lap. She clasped her hands around her youngest sister's waist and rocked her back and forth.

"I did everything," Amita said. "I swear on our mother's life I did everything to make him like me. He didn't like the smell of onions and garlic on my breath; I gave up all dishes that had traces of either. He said my anklets were too tinkly—those were his words—I took them off. He said he was a light sleeper, so I stayed away when he was taking his afternoon nap. What else could I have done?"

Sheela momentarily clamped her hand across Amita's mouth so as to stem the desperate flow.

After a long silence, Vasanti asked, "Did you show him the note?"

"And risk being thrown out of the house?"

"He wouldn't do that!" Vasanti's voice was small with disbelief. "You are his wife."

"In name only," Amita said.

"He wouldn't throw her out, would he?" Vasanti asked Sheela.

"He could if he wanted to."

Vasanti's eyes travelled to the iron bars that made up the triangles of the terrace balustrade, moved to the cracked and tarred stone underneath her feet, and settled on the silver ring that gripped her middle toe in a tight spiral. The knot in her stomach threatened to cut off her breath. She reached for the water on the table and poured herself a glass.

"He wouldn't dare throw her out." Nina's voice was sarcastic. "Scandal in the House of Chafékar? God forbid."

"Don't refer to the family with such disrespect. Remember that we are all Chafékar now," Sheela said.

Amita got off Sheela's lap and Nina took the rebuke in silence.

"So what's to be done?" Vasanti asked.

"Nothing." Sheela's voice was firm. "The woman can write Amita all the notes she wants; she can beg, plead, blackmail, but this is not Amita's problem. It is Yogesh's. Let him sort it out."

"I told you not to go into the afternoon sun," Baba said when they were in bed that night, reaching over and removing Vasanti's hand as she massaged her temple.

"I didn't," she said.

"Then what cause for a headache?"

She was silent.

"Vasanti?"

She started to turn away, but he placed his hand on her shoulder.

"You're angry because I cancelled our English lesson today."

She dropped her eyes. "What if you meet someone? In London." The words came out in a rush.

"What?"

"Another woman."

"Is that what you've been thinking?" She could hear laughter in his voice.

Tears rolled across the bridge of her nose. "What if you forget me and find someone else?"

"Of course I won't. What an absurd thing to say! Wasn't it only yesterday that you agreed to be sad no more and to make the best of the remaining time?"

But she had to ask one more time: "You promise?"

"Of course I promise! Now come here so we can properly seal that pledge."

~ ELEVEN ~

Towards early June, four months after the start of her English lessons, Vasanti began to feel optimistic. Her initial hopelessness turned into pride of achievement as words and their meanings started to fall into place, and she knew that one day she would attempt to read the spines of Baba's books. She might even post him brief notes written in English during his stay abroad.

The incident of Amita's letter was now a couple of weeks past, yet the pall cast by the other woman's communiqué dogged the wives still. Amita had set fire to the poisonous message and no servant girl had appeared bearing another. Nonetheless, she seemed to be in a constant state of dread: what if the woman were to appear in person?

Even if that happened, Sheela maintained, she was still

not Amita's problem to solve. She was Yogesh's headache, and if she was indeed carrying his child then it was up to him to buy her silence.

Vasanti was impressed by Sheela's composure.

"Maybe she's not even expecting," Nina said. "We have nothing to go on except this letter, which could have been written by anyone. Perhaps it's some business rival—not even a woman—who is trying to blackmail Yogesh through you."

"You are just saying that to make up for what you said earlier," Amita said.

"What did she say?" Sheela asked.

"Nothing!" Nina said, flushing.

"She said this is what I get for being proud that I bagged the best-looking husband of us three."

"It came out wrong," Nina said. "You know I didn't mean that."

"I don't know anything of the kind. In any case, I asked him last night."

Nina gasped.

"You said you wouldn't," Sheela said.

"You don't know what it's like for me. None of you do. You only think you understand . . . He says he knows no one with the initials T.L."

"See!" Nina said. "What did I tell you? The whole thing is a hoax."

"You are so gullible, Nina. He's lying, don't you see? All I know is that there *was* this woman and God only knows when she will be replaced by another."

Vasanti waited for Sheela to intervene, to challenge Amita's interpretation. But Sheela was silent, and all at once Vasanti had an eerie feeling that this incident was a mere layer, that there was much about the family that remained buried. She put the thought out of her mind; she wasn't ready for further secrets to be revealed.

That night, Vasanti showed Baba a book sheathed in brown paper. "I found this on the windowsill in the anteroom. It wasn't there yesterday."

"Nanasahib sent that," he said, without looking up.

Her fingers were poised to undo the twine. "May I?"

"Sure."

Inside was a leather-bound book, with embossed lettering etched into its cover and spine. She held it up. "What's the title?"

He translated it for her. "*How Green Was My Valley.*"

She opened the book and held up the inscription on the blank leaf preceding the title page. "What does it say?"

"*More than just a good read, Llewellyn does a superb job of feeding the soul.*"

"Your father wrote that?"

"Yes."

"I won't forget to place it inside your trunk."

"I have no intention of carrying it with me."

"Why not?"

"When I return we will read it together. Unless, of course, you become so good in English that you get a chance to look at it before I do."

"I will place it in your trunk."

"I'm warning you: if you do that, I will only remove it."

She set aside the tome and changed the subject. "Last week when I was at the temple, Guruji told me that your mother would observe Monday fasts. I thought I should too. Today is my first day of keeping fasts."

"That's why you didn't have a biscuit along with your morning tea."

"Guruji also told me that you were with your mother when she . . ."

"Yes, I was."

"He said her passing away was very peaceful."

"It was."

"Do you ever think of that time, or does it hurt too much?" Vasanti's voice was scratchy.

"I think about it sometimes and, no, it doesn't hurt. Not any more. It all happened so long ago."

He lifted his quilt and waited for her to lean against him before beginning to talk about his mother.

~

The day after Baba had finished writing the last paper of his matriculation exam some eight years earlier, Nanasahib sent a message for his son to visit him in his office. Baba hadn't been in the office since the afternoon his father had granted his request to study law. As before, Nanasahib was seated at his desk, and when he turned around, Baba noticed that his upper lip and temples were shiny.

"You wanted to see me?"

"Come and sit down. How did your exams go?"

"All right. A couple of papers were difficult but I was expecting them to be."

Nanasahib removed a hand towel from the back of his chair; he mopped his face with it and folded it neatly across his lap.

"Your mother needs a holiday," he said. "A little respite from this pre-monsoon heat. I'm thinking of sending her to some hill station. I want you to go along to keep her company."

The suggestion was so unexpected and Nanasahib's manner so strangely nervous that Baba was alarmed. "Is Aai all right?"

"There's no easy way of putting this: your mother has been coughing up blood this past month."

Dread seized Baba.

Nanasahib left his chair and stood looking out the

window. "Tomorrow I want you to accompany her to Chikaldhara."

"Why Chikaldhara?" Baba said, addressing his father's back.

Nanasahib turned around. "Dr. Gadgil thinks the mountain air will do her good."

"What's wrong with Aai?"

"Tuberculosis."

Just the previous year, a boy in Baba's school had died of the very same disease. "What medicines has Dr. Gadgil prescribed?" he asked, his mouth drying up even as he spoke.

"None."

"What do you mean?"

"There are no medicines for TB. One can only employ measures to lessen the symptoms. Tonics, healthy food, fresh mountain air."

After giving Baba a minute or two to digest the unpalatable, Nanasahib informed his youngest of the arrangements he had made for them to stay at a recommended guesthouse in Chikaldhara. Baba was to look after his mother for as long he was able to keep her there. There were no other instructions. Heartsick and anxious as he felt, Baba nevertheless promised his father that he would nurse Ramabai back to health.

~

On the morning they were to leave, Nanasahib drove in early from Pegasus and reminded the driver repeatedly that he was not to drive fast, especially on hairpin bends where accidents were known to happen. Her three older sons helped Ramabai into the car while admonishing her that she was not to exert herself and that she was to eat well and do everything that would make her feel better in no time. Their entreaties were kind and solicitous and brought a lump to Baba's throat.

The journey to Chikaldhara was a lengthy one and it was several hours before they began their ascent into the hills. The air then became refreshingly cool, and Baba could tell by her animated expression that Ramabai was pleased to be making this excursion. The car chugged up the winding roads, and at last they were at the guesthouse. As they passed through the open gate, Baba noticed the large pots of flowering frangipani lining the driveway. He pointed them out to Ramabai. She lowered her window and at once the car became redolent with their scent.

A host of servants came forward to greet them and Ramabai said she would like to stretch her legs before taking refreshments. Later, she ate dinner with a robust appetite.

The following morning, Baba joined her in the veranda as she cradled a cup of tea while watching chattering bulbuls swoop in and out of bushes less than ten feet away. She had never looked so beautiful, or so serene.

Nanasahib had told him that there were many horse trails in Chikaldhara but Baba did not wish to leave Ramabai that very first day, and so he stayed in the house, and in the afternoon he kept an eye on her as she rested. He fell asleep in his chair and came awake to the loud beating of a tom-tom. His mother was no longer on her bed. He joined her underneath the porch where she was observing a crowd gathered at the end of the driveway.

"What's happening?" he said, but she shook her head.

He walked to the gate and out into the narrow dirt lane, pushing his way through a bank of children and bigger youth, amongst them women and girls. As he watched, a garishly dressed trio ambled towards him, large baskets balanced on their heads, capacious cloth bags hanging from their shoulders. Someone said, "Sahib, ask Assamese family to put on show. They are best in the region."

He turned to Ramabai, cupped his hands around his mouth and hollered, "Magicians!"

When he turned around, the painted troupe was upon him. The oldest bawled at the tom-tom-beating youngest to belt up. The ensuing silence caused Baba's ears to pop. The second oldest came forward and held a lemon under Baba's nose. He brandished as though out of thin air a switchblade and brought it down on the lemon, and before Baba could follow with his eyes the intricacies of his actions, he held a bowl in his left palm and squeezed into it the fruit. The juice as it left the lemon was a bloody red: Baba felt a chilling sensation creep down his spine.

He turned towards the guesthouse. The gate had been thrown open and the servants had brought forward two chairs. Ramabai lowered herself into one, and Baba sat in the other. To the beat of the tom-tom, the oldest magician pretended to part a curtain. His grandson came forward and began the performance with a juggling act, keeping up in the air no less than seven balls made of tightly wound string. Next, the boy threw himself into rapid cartwheels, hands and feet touching the ground only momentarily, his athleticism culminating in a triple somersault.

For the final act, he balanced a glass of water on the blunt top of a long stick clutched tightly between his teeth. He removed the stick from his mouth and made way for his father, who was flapping in the air a large green handkerchief. The man squatted on his haunches and spread the cloth on the packed earth before him. He began a series of incantations and after drawing his hands across the top of the cloth, he snatched away the taffeta, shaped it into a bag, reached into it, and pulled out a white dove, which he threw up into the air. The bird circled the gathering a few times before perching itself on the branch of a nearby tree.

Baba glanced down to see the grandfather holding a serpent: it looked long, thin and sinister. Clutching it with one hand, the old man shrugged out of his clothes and flung his outer garments away from his body. Wearing nothing but a loincloth, he deposited the snake on the ground and covered it with yellow silk. He drew his hands wildly over the cloth, barely touching it as he uttered more cantations, and when his voice reached its highest pitch, he snatched away the cloth to reveal there was nothing underneath it. The seated people rose to their feet in case the reptile had slithered their way.

Baba jumped up as well and looked down at his mother. She said, "I'm quite all right."

By now an empty flowerpot had been placed in the middle of the lane. The grandson filled it with watered earth. Next, his father came forward and dropped a few seeds into it, announcing that they were mango seeds. He lifted the flowerpot and rested it on a bamboo tripod, afterwards covering the stand and pot with a large cloth. He circled the covered pot slowly, allowing his robes to envelop it at each turn. After a minute or so, the man stepped back, removing the white cloth, and there in front of them was a mango tree, three feet in height, with shiny emerald leaves. The audience clapped loudly.

Baba scanned the trees. The dove, which had been grooming itself on a branch a few minutes earlier, was no longer there.

The crowd began to disperse. When the magicians were done tidying, they approached Ramabai. Each reached down and touched her feet. She placed some money in the grand-father's hand, and said, "Those were very clever tricks you performed."

"Sleights of hand, Ma," the old trickster said. "All illusion, just like Life."

After dinner that night, sitting in the veranda, the moon a golden crescent in a remarkably low sky, Ramabai told Baba she felt at peace, adding, "Given a choice, I could stay here forever."

"But you wouldn't." Baba was alarmed.

"It's tempting."

"It may be tempting. But you can't live here permanently. I won't let you."

"Sometimes, my son," she said, "you act as though you are ten years old and not sixteen. You are almost a grown man now. You will marry one day and raise your own children."

"But until I do, I need you to be at Chafékar Wadi."

"Well, you don't need to worry. Even though I may wish to live here, I know I cannot. And do you know why? Because it is my duty as a parent to look after my sons. It is the same reason why your father continues to work hard, so that future generations may inherit a thriving concern. He accedes to your wish to study law because it is his responsibility to support and encourage you."

Baba was listening attentively. He couldn't remember

the last time Ramabai had referred to Nanasahib in such specific terms.

"One day, you will be a father. And just like your father before you, you will also stand by your children. You will feed them and nurture them and provide for their needs. You will accept their frailties along with their strengths, and as you guide them through life you will harbour for them unstinting love. Will you promise to do all of that? Even if it is difficult?"

"I promise."

After a while Ramabai began to yawn. Baba held out his hand to her and said, "I've asked the houseboy to open the windows in your room. Your maidservant told me you were perspiring all night."

"That's not a detail she should be telling you, or anyone else for that matter."

"I asked her how your night had gone, so don't go scolding her. Also, I'm sending in a glass of milk. Don't forget to drink it."

"Yes, Baba!"

Sometime in the middle of the night, the high moon casting a weak light through the window bars, Baba came awake to a loud and persistent knocking. The panicked voice of Ramabai's maidservant was telling him to hurry to his mother's room. He pushed past the woman and found his mother lying on her bed. Her eyes were closed, her mouth had lost colour, her breathing was shallow, her hands lay life-less by her side.

The houseboys were standing by.

"Go fetch a doctor," Baba shouted at them.

They rushed out of the room.

"Bai collapsed as I was helping her back from the bath-room," the maid said. "The servants picked her up and laid her on the bed."

"How long ago was that?" There was iron in Baba's voice.

"A minute or so, that's all. I called out to them before coming to your room because I couldn't bear to leave her on the floor."

Baba crouched by Ramabai's bed and took her hand in his: her fingernails were opal. She opened her eyes briefly—they were milky. She had recognized him; he tightened his grip. Now her lips and fingernails were blue.

He forced himself to speak slowly. "Aai? The doctor will be here any minute. Can you hear me? Aai? Open your eyes."

Her eyelids fluttered open: her eyes had rolled back into their sockets.

Some twenty minutes later he was still clutching her limp hand in the two of his when the gateman rushed into the room and announced that there was no resident doctor in Chikaldhara; the nearest lived on the plains, miles away.

He sat by her bedside, his eyes hollowed out but dry, until the first of the family—his brothers and Nanasahib—arrived in Chikaldhara, weary, speechless and shaken. Only then did he sit in the veranda, the noon sun slanting into his body, tears falling into his cup. There was no birdsong now: the bushes were silent and still.

Ramabai was forty-two years old.

Nanasahib came and sat beside him in the chair. Without looking at his father, Baba said, "You knew, didn't you, that she was dying? And yet you asked me to accompany her. You were too busy like always and didn't think twice before thrusting your responsibility onto me."

After a long pause, Nanasahib held Baba's gaze and quietly said, "I didn't know she was dying. In fact I had every expectation that she would get better. I know we will all miss her sorely, and you will need every ounce of your courage to overcome your loss. But you have inherited your mother's fortitude, so I shall not worry too much."

Baba was silent, disarmed by his father's sincerity.

Nanasahib continued, moving forward in his chair, "Before I leave you to make the arrangements, there is something I wish to say. Difficult as it is for you to believe me right now, I want you to know that of all the people in the world, you are the one person she would have wanted by her side."

Baba shrugged off his father's preposterous suggestion

and lifted Ramabai's prayer book from where it was lying on the table. He carried it to his bedroom and sat in the windowsill before opening it to the inscription his mother had written on its very first page.

"Her prayer book is in the top drawer of my desk," Baba told Vasanti now.

After fetching it, Vasanti opened it and read aloud: "It is no use asking why the small stream is not the mighty Ganges, or why the sparrow does not fan its feathers like the peacock, or why the coconut palm does not provide shade as does the banyan tree. Each is what it is and so it is with mankind: all His creation, we are what we are."

Looking at Baba's sad expression Vasanti thought how close father and son must have been for Nanasahib to have trusted Baba so completely to take care of his ailing mother; and how acutely Baba must have suffered when he was required to face her demise all by himself. She wondered whether Baba's deep reluctance to talk about his father, the wariness that coloured his expression, the tension that entered his body at any mention of Nanasahib, were due to the fact that after all these years, he was still very angry and hadn't yet forgiven his father for everything he had put Baba through when he'd suggested he accompany Ramabai to Chikaldhara.

"I wish my mother, your mother, my father, that they were all alive," Vasanti said. "Why did God have to take them away so soon?"

He put his arm around her and pulled her close. "I'll make it up to you. You'll see. When I return from England we will have children, lots of them."

She looked up and searched his face. "Children?" Her eyes were wet with hope.

"Three, maybe four."

They lay silently for a while.

"May I use your mother's prayer book while you are gone?"

Nodding, he closed his eyes.

Vasanti watched him for a while, hoping he knew that now that he had shared with her the details of Ramabai's death, they would never be forgotten. She said a prayer for all the lost souls before falling asleep.

~ TWELVE ~

AT LAST ONLY TWO DAYS remained until Baba was to set sail. Nanasahib sent word that he would meet his son in Bombay, where the journey to Liverpool would truly begin. Relatives and friends had been dropping into the house to say farewell the entire week. Most of the guests hid their anxious thoughts, wishing Baba a fruitful journey. However, a couple of older uncles suggested that it wasn't too late to set aside his foolishness and change his plans. They insisted that nothing would be lost and on the contrary everything gained if only he would rethink his decision to leave.

But his mother's brother, Bhikumama, said, "The arrangements have all been made so the only thing to do now is to wish Baba Godspeed. When we next see him he will be a Barrister-at-Law. Think what honour he will bring to his country, to his family, to us."

Upon hearing his uncle's words, a bitter gorge rose inside Baba. If only he could share with Bhikumama the real reason he was leaving for England, divulge to him the scandalous facts about his father, details that could ruin the so-called honour and prestige of the Chafékar family. When he had chanced upon the truth at Pegasus, a few months prior to his marriage to Vasanti, life at home had become all of a sudden unbearable, triggering into motion the plan to leave for England, a plan that would allow him to escape having to confront his father's secret, if not forever, at least for a while.

Less than a year previously, and a couple of months before Baba's twenty-fourth birthday, Nagpur announced that it would host the region's Festival of Plays. An enthusiastic follower of the theatre, Nanasahib sent word to the family that instead of commuting from his stud farm, he would spend the middle two weeks of October at Chafékar Wadi, from where it would be more convenient for him to attend all the events. Word of his extended stay got out and almost as soon as his car came to a standstill underneath the porch, the house came alive with friends and relatives, and Sheela, Amita and Nina began to plan menus and strategies to feed all the guests.

Baba made it a point to return home early, and nothing gave him greater pleasure than drinking tea with his father by the poolside at six o' clock every morning, when the rest of the house would only be stirring. One day, while they were watching the sun rise from behind the jungle, flooding its canopy with a misty glow, Baba informed him that the father–son doubles tennis tournament at the Gymkhana was slated to begin in December and asked whether he could enter their names in the draw. Nanasahib was immediately agreeable, and Baba was pleasantly surprised. The last time they had taken part in the tournament was when Ramabai was alive. Baba reminded his father of this and for a few minutes they shared with fondness the memory of her laughing and coaching them with hand signals from the sidelines during the games.

There was a large get-together the night before Nanasahib left Chafékar Wadi to return to Pegasus. His sisters were all present, and complained boisterously that his two-day visits were much too short and urged him to come down to the Wadi for at least a fortnight every couple of months. Nanasahib looked doubtful, but said he would consider longer stays.

Chafékar Wadi felt bereft and discarded after his departure, and the one person who was pleased to have quiet descend was the accountant, whose harried and demanding job it was to enter into his cumbersome ledger the domestic expenses incurred by the family the previous year. It took him a week to finish his task and once it was completed, he sent a message that the ledger book was ready to be placed in front of the gods. Baba accompanied the man to the temple.

After offering up a prayer of thanksgiving, the accountant said, "Suresh sahib is in Delhi. Given that to be the case I'll need your father to sign off on the accounts."

"He's not here," Baba said. "But I'm sure he won't mind if I sign on his behalf."

"That won't do." The man was truculent. "You will have to find someone to take the ledger to him."

Without giving it any thought, Baba said, "He's at the farm. I'll take it down myself."

It was several years since he had visited Pegasus. There was a hill in its vicinity that had a natural waterfall and a man-made lake. Baba hoped to persuade his father to go riding with him to its summit. He called Nanasahib to discuss with him this plan. However, the phone connection kept breaking and he couldn't get through. Consequently, he arrived at Pegasus unannounced.

The stables were bustling. The trainers and the stable hands were unfamiliar, yet they doffed their grimy caps to him, most likely recognizing the resemblance between father and son. He watched the horses at exercise, and after the animals were returned to their stalls, walked to the farmhouse, along the narrow bicycle path through the centre of which ran a line of grass, full and tufted like a horse's mane. He pushed against the wooden gate but it was latched from the inside. He called out for someone to open it, and when nobody came forward, he vaulted over and went to the side entrance, noticing with relief that Nanasahib's car was parked in the garage. Thirsty, he entered the kitchen. It was empty. Most likely the servants were sleeping off the heat.

He tiptoed up the stairs so as not to disturb his father, in case he was also resting. The door to Nanasahib's room was open; there was no one inside. Wondering where his father could be, he heard a splash of water and the sound of a man clearing his throat. He crossed the room and glanced out of the window overlooking the back garden. Directly below, sitting underneath the shifting shade of a mango tree, dressed in a thin pair of cotton shorts, his father was dangling his feet in a shallow artificial pond shaped like a horse's head. Another man was lying along the pond's narrow ledge, his head resting on Nanasahib's lap. The man's body, dressed only in a flimsy loincloth, was a burnished brown; a wide, gold chain glinted around his neck. So intimate was the scene, and so unexpected its nature that Baba felt a violent clutch deep inside his body. His heart beating wildly, he turned away, and perhaps sensing a movement above him, Nanasahib looked up. Their eyes locked and in that split moment filled with anguished communication, father and son both knew that their world would never again be the same.

Breaking gaze, Baba slid down the wall, pressing his fists into his forehead. He heard the soft murmur of voices and before his father could come into the house, he stumbled to his feet, bounded down the stairs, vaulted over the latched gate and sprinted down the path to the stables, thinking he would be able to control the urge to throw up if only he could get away.

His driver was chewing on a shaft of grass, watching the horses that were now tossing their heads and stomping their hooves in a futile attempt to rid their bodies of the buzzing, attacking flies. He asked the man to leave the accounts ledger in the office, and to instruct the stable manager to give it to his father to sign when he came down that evening.

"Be sure to tell the manager that there is no urgency, no need to disturb Nanasahib right away. And if my father doesn't visit the stables this evening he can be shown the ledger whenever he does."

The driver entered the office and stepped out within a minute, followed by a youth.

"The manager is not in, the boy says. He's at the main house. I left the book on Nanasahib's desk."

"Is the stable manager new?" Baba asked.

"He's been with us for more than ten years, Sahib," someone said.

Baba thought there was a smirk on the youth's face but he couldn't be sure.

Dodging the driver's perplexed expression, for Baba had told the man that he would be spending the entire day and perhaps the night at Pegasus, he wrenched open the car door and got in.

There was very little traffic on the road, and as he sat in the cross-current of winds, staring at the procession of trees as they rushed by, Baba knew that the image of magnificent breeding horses would forever be tainted in his memory with the secret he'd stumbled into that afternoon.

The repugnant picture of the two men wrapped in intimacy beside the horse-head pond kept Baba awake that night. And all at once the reason why his father had chosen to live away from Chafékar Wadi became lucidly clear. Something told him that his mother had known about Nanasahib's proclivity all along, and that she had suffered because of it. She had been bitter when he was younger, with a caustic tongue, sometimes even flying into rages; then, as he grew older, he recalled family elders remarking that Rama's acidity had melted away, to be replaced by a much calmer and admirable state of poise. He wondered now whether her change of heart had anything to do with her coming to terms with Nanasahib's disloyalty. But whatever it was that prompted and allowed her to reconcile with her peculiar reality, Baba knew that *he* would never forgive Nanasahib—much less accept or understand him.

He pondered on the time after Ramabai's passing away, when family and friends had come to Chafékar Wadi to pay their condolences. All said how strong and tough she had been, how accepting of her lot. He had thought then that they were referring to her final illness, but speculated now that it may have been the abnormal circumstances of her marriage they were thinking about. He was mortified to think that his immediate family—there was no question in his mind that his brothers knew what he had only just discovered—and perhaps the whole world saw Nanasahib for what he truly was, and it was only he, his mother's darling, Nanasahib's grey-eyed look-alike, who had been spared the truth. Why had Ramabai kept this secret from him? Yet, all the signs were there; if only he had had the maturity to see them: the separate living quarters, the separate lives, Nanasahib's frequent absences from home, his mother's unnatural piety. How could he have missed the meaning behind them all?

But in his more lucid moments, when he could get himself to become an advocate for facts, he recognized that there was no evidence to suggest that anyone beyond his immediate family knew Nanasahib's secret. As far as society was concerned, his standing was decidedly unblemished: he was highly respected, admired for his physical beauty, sought out for his liberal advice, praised for his Midas touch. It was known within family circles that he was a generous man, and indigent relatives could approach him in times of need. No, Nanasahib had concealed his double life so securely, he had been so discreet that even his most favourite son was on the other side of those tightly fitted drapes.

When he walked down the stairs the following day, the signed ledger was on the table in the vestibule. He wondered with a nervous flutter whether Nanasahib was back. The servants informed him that the ledger had been delivered by a courier along with a note that said that Nanasahib would return to Chafékar Wadi in a fortnight, when the traditional ceremony honouring Chafékar ancestors would be performed.

On the day Nanasahib was expected, Baba returned home late, but when they came face to face on the stairs the following morning, Nanasahib smiled at his youngest with the openness of former days, his face collapsing only at the sight of Baba's wounded expression. Baba retreated to his room until the start of the religious ceremony, which he could not escape.

In the evening, after the last of the visiting relatives had departed, Nanasahib summoned Baba to his study and told him to take a seat. Baba said he preferred to stand. Without making any reference to what had passed at Pegasus, Nanasahib informed his son that the senior partner in the law firm where he had arranged for Baba to obtain tort experience wished now to meet up with him. Baba narrowed his eyes and Nanasahib quickly added that Bhikumama—Baba's mentor and Ramabai's brother—was agreeable to this scheme.

His eyes unwavering, Baba ignored his father's words and said, "I've decided to go to London, to be accepted to the bar. I talked this over with Christopher the last time he was here and he thinks the Inner Temple will be pleased to accept me. I've been making inquiries about ships sailing to Liverpool."

"But there is a war being fought and much of London has been bombed."

"I don't care."

"But the Inner Temple. Does it stand or has it been razed?" Nanasahib patted his brow with a handkerchief.

Throat locked with sudden tears, Baba could hardly speak.

"I don't know."

"Let us presume it remains undamaged. Do you know whether it is accepting new students?"

Nanasahib's conversational tone felt condescending and Baba was incensed.

"I have made up my mind to leave and nothing is going to stop me."

"But why now, Baba? Why not wait until after the war?"

"You very well know the answer to that."

Ignoring Baba's response, Nanasahib said, "No wars last forever. Go later, when London is safe. I never stood in the way of your law career, did I? All I'm asking now is that you wait a bit." He moved his shaking hands to his lap where Baba could not see them. "Have you talked over your going away with Bhiku?"

"No, I haven't. And if you rope in Bhikumama, his interference will only strengthen my resolve to leave." Baba had never before used this hostile tone with his father, and he grabbed the back of a chair to steady himself.

After a long pause, Nanasahib said, "I thought you knew about me, about us."

So taken aback was Baba by his father's veiled reference to the man that his heart began to pound and the blood rushed away from his skin.

"A very long time ago, your brothers—just like you—stumbled onto my secret. I thought they might have shared it with you."

He wished to God that his brothers had informed him right away.

Nanasahib's eyes were pleading. "Can't you forget what you saw? Can't we carry on like before? For all practical purposes, it doesn't matter one way or the other—"

His mother had died so young. Baba could only imagine how much she must have suffered, the strength of her loneliness, her pain.

"But it mattered to Aai, or do you not think so? How could you submit her to such disloyalty? And humiliation."

Nanasahib flinched. "You must know that however things stood between me and your mother, I always looked after her needs. And as far as you children are concerned, my heart has always been yours. You know that. There is no disloyalty there."

"Does anyone else know?" he asked.

"All I can say is that I have been very careful to keep my private life private, and away from prying eyes."

Repelled once again by the memory of the manager's hand encircling Nanasahib's ankle, Baba knew he could not continue to live here as though nothing had happened.

His tone no longer pleading, Nanasahib said, "I cannot grant you permission to go abroad."

Baba gave a bitter laugh. "I'm not asking for your permission."

"Don't let my life affect your decisions, Baba. You could get killed. Consider what your mother would have advised."

"She was dead to you while she was living. So don't go bringing her into the conversation now. Blackmail me with her name once more and I will cut myself off from the family and you will never see me again."

Nanasahib swallowed, his eyes filling with sadness. He slumped back in his chair and covered his face with his hands. Baba started to move to the door.

His father's tone was resigned. "You leave me with little choice but to accede to your plans. It is a long journey—and

I don't just mean the sea crossing. If you think you can undertake it without making proper arrangements, you are more naive than I thought." Nanasahib had already regained his composure. "Without my help, life will be intolerable there. Even with my help . . ."

Baba stepped forward. "Aren't you worried about a scandal? What will people say if one day word gets out?" The thought of wagging tongues and his late mother's and the family's name getting dragged into a vortex of dishonour was reprehensible.

Nanasahib looked at him gravely, then dropped his eyes.

Angered by his father's wretched intransigence, Baba wanted more than anything for Nanasahib to say that what he had stumbled into at Pegasus was a mere aberration, a temporary veering off the road.

"I'll reconsider my decision only if you promise to sell Pegasus," he said. "Come home to Chafékar Wadi and forget everything else."

Nanasahib's mouth curled into a twisted smile but his voice was gentle. "Unfortunately, I cannot do as you ask of me. I would do anything to keep you here. But not that."

"You are choosing that man over your own family?"

"It is not a question of choice, Baba. If only you understood that, then perhaps one day you'd be less likely to condemn."

"You have betrayed us, all of us."

Nanasahib rubbed his eyes with his fists, then said, "You do plan to return to Nagpur, do you not?"

Baba did not reply. He walked to the door and grabbed its handle.

"Will you tell your brothers about your decision to leave, or shall I?"

"I'll tell them."

His father was pushing back in his chair when Baba left the room, wishing he could turn back the clock, wishing that the obtuse, stickler of an accountant had accepted Baba's signature and not forced him to obtain Nanasahib's instead.

Baba wrote his brothers a note explaining his decision to study abroad and sent it to them at the Mills the following afternoon. Right away they called a meeting in Nanasahib's study, and after dinner that night, Baba sat down in the spotlight of their shocked, disbelieving glares. They had always envied his nerve to opt out of the family business and were probably thinking that they would rather be damned than support his wish to further that project now. It would not be until much later when, unable to acknowledge and reciprocate their goodwill, he would realize that they cared for him deeply and that their objections meant they were terrified for his safety inside a country at war.

When Nanasahib took his place behind his desk, they turned to their father and demanded that he put his foot down and forbid Baba from thrusting his head into the lion's den that was England. Nanasahib said that he had tried his best to dissuade his youngest but as far as he could understand, Baba's mind was made up and there was nothing he could do or say to prohibit him, let alone get him to postpone his decision to leave.

"Cut off his funding," Suresh said.

"I would still go," Baba replied.

"Without money?" Suresh laughed. "You wouldn't survive a day. No family influence where you're going. No one to extend you credit, no one will even know who you are, or care."

It took every bit of strength in Baba's body not to respond. Yet, they were suggesting something that would definitely put a wedge in his plans. Faced with this new, unanticipated obstacle he did what came to him naturally— he remained silent.

"Baba is very determined," Nanasahib said. "As you can all see." He turned to Suresh. "I want you to help him with the arrangements."

Baba hardened his heart. Nanasahib probably thought he could buy a change of resolve with generous acquiescence, but he was wrong. That morning he had received a letter from his father imploring him to reconsider his decision to leave. Baba had torn it up.

The second oldest, Ramesh, was speaking to their father. "I don't think you should let him have his way. Especially because he insists on going against the wishes of the entire family."

"What would you have me do?" Nanasahib said. "Put him under lock?" His tone was weary.

Suresh said, "Our father wants me to help you go abroad so you may be admitted to the bar and I give him my word that I will. But if I am required to compromise, surely I have the right to expect the same of you?"

"As long as you don't ask me to reconsider my decision to leave," Baba said.

"Agreed."

"So, what do you want from me?"

"It doesn't look as though our father has told you, but we accepted only recently a marriage proposal that was made to you some time ago."

Baba's body went rigid; his face was flooded with heat. "What marriage proposal? You cannot agree to anything without asking me first."

Suresh said, "You are twenty-four, of marriageable age."

"Besides," Yogesh said, "I don't remember anybody seeking our consent before our marriage plans were finalized."

Baba turned to Nanasahib. "When were you going to tell me?"

"Yesterday evening, when we met," his father replied.

His brothers did not see Nanasahib's uneasiness, their eyes were so tightly fixed on him.

"Then why didn't you?" Baba demanded.

"I thought I'd save that news for another time. I knocked on your door this morning but you had gone riding. In the afternoon I sent for you but this time you were attending court."

"So you see, Baba," Ramesh said. "All marriage plans have been finalized. Suresh wrote the girl's uncle only a fortnight ago. If you had shared with us what was inside your head about going to England, we wouldn't have said we were agreeable to the match now, would we?"

The important thing, Baba knew, was to remain calm: he might be trapped, but he was nowhere near beaten. "I'll agree to the marriage," he said, "but only after I return. We can, if the girl's side wishes, do the engagement ceremony before I leave."

"That won't do." Suresh shook his head. "The girl lives in Poona and her mother died when she was three years old and it's only recently that her father passed away. Her uncle, whose responsibility she is now, wants no delay. You will have to marry her before you leave."

His brothers filed out of the room.

Baba looked at Nanasahib. There were dark shadows of regret inside his eyes. Baba softened his gaze: it still wasn't too late. All Nanasahib had to do was reconsider his decision not to sell Pegasus, and return home to Chafékar Wadi. But his father remained silent.

Filled with anguish, Baba rushed out of the room. He wished to heaven that the confounded girl the family had chosen for him did not exist.

It was ten o'clock at night by the time the last visitor left. Baba was already in bed when Vasanti exited the dressing room, washed and changed. She moved towards the centre of the bed and pressed her body into his side. He switched off the lamp.

"I want to say a couple of things," he said.

She buried her face in his shoulder.

"Postal service between England and India is severely disrupted. So if you don't hear from me right away or if there is a gap in communication, don't any of you assume the worst."

"But you will send us your permanent address as soon as you have it."

"Of course." He made his second request. "Will you write to me?"

"Yes, but only if you write first."

"Done."

He placed his arm around her waist and pulled her on top of him. Lowering her mouth onto his and slipping her small palms underneath his neck, she kissed him deeply.

"So this is your sweet way of bidding me farewell," he teased.

Looking into his grey-blue eyes, she uttered solemnly the words that would ring in his ears for months and years to come: "I began to say goodbye the very day you told me you were leaving. That was also the day I began awaiting your return."

~ THIRTEEN ~

IN THE MORNING BABA PERFORMED a short puja in the temple. Later, while his luggage was being loaded into the car, the household gathered in the driveway to bid him farewell. Vasanti stood to one side surrounded by her sisters-in-law, and the face she held up to the world was brave and composed, just the way she had promised him it would be.

At the railway station in Nagpur, there were more farewells; and when he reached the Bombay docks Vasanti's uncle, Vishnupant, and cousin, Keshav, were waiting for him in the departure lounge. He recognized them instantly and moved towards them, oddly glad that they had come to see him off.

"We couldn't let you leave without wishing you our very

best," Keshav said, placing a garland of roses around Baba's neck. "How's Vasanti?"

"Not too happy at the moment, as you can imagine."

They moved to one side as soldiers filed past, two abreast, their kit bags flung over their shoulders.

Vishnupant turned to Baba. "A word of caution, if I may?"

Baba nodded.

"I know you are leaving us to become a barrister and I commend your ambition. It would be wise, however, never to forget that your sole priority at all times is to remain safe. We want you to return in one piece."

"Also," Keshav said, "if London is bombed again, or threatened in any way, or for any reason things don't work out, don't hesitate—just return home."

"I will do that . . ."

After taking leave of Vasanti's relatives, Baba walked along the quay, searching the docks for Nanasahib. Eventually he saw his father standing at the bottom of the gangway, hat in hand, his clothes impeccable as always; but dark creases ringed his eyes.

Heart beating unsteadily, Baba looked away; they had not had a proper conversation in months and he didn't know with what words to address his father. Before he could formulate a greeting, Nanasahib quickly moved forward and placing his hands on his son's shoulders, clasped him to his chest.

Stepping back, Nanasahib said, "It is inauspicious to ask someone to cancel a journey at the very last minute, so I won't. But I want you to know how sorry I am that it has come to this. I never meant to cause you or anyone in the family any suffering or harm."

Baba bent down and touched his father's feet, but no sooner had he straightened than he regretted this ingrained impulse. Struck by anger, he could scarcely believe that Nanasahib had chosen to offer an apology at this irrevocable stage.

Ignoring Baba's fury, Nanasahib leaned forward and clasping Baba's right hand in both of his, said, "Have a safe journey, my son, and don't forget to send us a telegram as soon as you have reached England, and keep us well informed of your academic progress." His father's tone was uncharacteristically pleading.

Disentangling his hand, Baba made a gesture to the coolie carrying his luggage to follow him. He waved feebly in the direction of his father and purposefully walked away.

Once installed in his cabin Baba removed the rose garland from around his neck and hung it behind the door. He went back on deck and watched the land recede, the distance between him and everything familiar increasing by the minute. Now that he was finally on his way, the sense of anticipation, of adventure, of new beginnings that he had discussed with Christopher while formulating future plans for studying in London were subsumed by regret, self-doubt and an insatiable longing for Vasanti. Gazing mindlessly into the breathing, shivering ocean, he shrugged off a feeling of doom and renewed his pledge to make the most of their separation.

Mostly there were soldiers on board, and a common meeting place for the handful of non-servicemen soon became the upper deck. On the very first day he met a group of American missionaries who were returning to the United States after spending several years in South India. The Americans were an outgoing, sociable lot and unreservedly delighted when they realized he spoke fluent English. Baba at first found them a pleasant antidote to his homesickness but over time became bored by their zeal to share with him their minutest impressions of India. Consequently, he soon began spending most of his afternoons in his cabin, even on occasion ordering his meals to be served there. He preferred to go on deck in the early mornings when all was solitude and quiet, the spectacle of the sun levitating from a brightening sea ever wondrous and pleasing. On these occasions his thoughts were consumed by the possible reason for the untimely apology offered by his father. Perhaps Nanasahib was attempting to ease his conscience in the event of something untoward happening to Baba; his apology made, there would be no guilt or regret afterwards. But much as he tried to paint his father as someone who was self-serving and devious, Baba knew that this picture was patently false.

Around midnight a week or so after the ship had left the Bombay docks, there was an urgent knocking on Baba's cabin door. A man in fatigues told him that he would be required to do lookout duty for a serviceman who had taken ill. Baba followed the soldier on deck, where a life jacket and a pair of binoculars were thrust into his hands. The ship observed strict blackout and he was led in the dark past the artillery to one of the anti-aircraft guns mounted in an open turret. He was introduced to a seaman named Bill, and told that he would do lookout duty alongside him until the next change of guard. Faced with this crucial task, Baba for the first time felt something akin to panic. He kept his eyes peeled, nervous in case Bill dozed off and he, Baba, missed something significant. Would he be able to distinguish the lights of enemy aircraft against the backdrop of the stars? Would he hear the drone of their engines above the noise of the battering wind? The sea looked inky and dangerous. What use his vigilance if they were torpedoed from below? He thanked the dazzling heavens that Vasanti was not with him.

As it turned out, they were far removed from enemy action, and when he was relieved of duty he went starboard and gazed into the water, and it was there that he caught the first glimmer of the sun, in the furrows of the wake of their gliding ship. He reflected that even though Vasanti was constantly in his thoughts, time did not drag nor was there a continual burden inside his heart. As the journey got underway, he looked forward to meeting Christopher, to taking in the sights of London, battered as they may be, and the thought of returning to Nagpur a barrister filled him with pride. And now that he was crossing the oceans against all odds, he could not help but think that it was Destiny guiding him. He all at once remembered something that his mother was given to repeat: *everything but everything is written.* He wished she were alive to see him achieve his dream.

His mood changed as the ship rounded the Cape of Good Hope. Seasick and miserable, he paced the narrow, claustrophobic corridors hour after hour, the pores of his skin clogged with brackish air. He was almost relieved—because it meant he was nearing the end of his four-week voyage—when days afterwards, the vessel moved north along Africa's west coast and the atmosphere aboard the ship became grim. The choppy, cold waters were infested with submarines now and everyone—even the children on board—fell silent. The odd time, Baba thought he could spot a battleship on the horizon. The stormy weather went into further decline as they approached Liverpool, and by the time Baba sighted land, his mouth was ashen with cold, his nostrils felt raw and there were purple shadows underneath his eyes.

~

The pewter grey water was reflecting the murky sky when Baba set foot on British soil. Still buoyed by his safe arrival at last, he surveyed his surroundings with enthusiastic curiosity. This, then, was the land of Shakespeare, Blake, Dickens, Chesterton, Doyle, Christie and Maugham. He waited for some kind of stirring, perhaps a sense of awe; but there was no feeling of familiarity, or kinship, merely cold and rain. He reminded himself not to judge a book by its cover, that this was a country at war: the signs were everywhere. Vigilant soldiers guarded the docks, anti-aircraft guns pointed long, metallic fingers at the clouds and plump sandbags were set out in neat rows alongside brick buildings. Dour and dishevelled, middle-aged dockworkers looked as though they hadn't slept in days, and Baba let his glance linger on them even as he walked by: he had never seen white manual workers, and the sight of an Englishman belonging to the labouring class was unexpected and novel. The men called out to each other and the English they spoke was undecipherable, and when he asked to be shown the way to the railway station, he was guided more by their gestures than by their words.

The journey to London was long with many unscheduled stops. A cloudburst had flooded the tracks, making it too wet and windy to step outside during halts; and although at one such stop he was tempted to stretch his legs and clear his lungs of the cigarette smoke that hung inside the compartment, he noticed with dismay that no other passengers were budging from their seats. Nevertheless, he went and stood by the closed door and peered out of its grimy window. The trees alongside the railway line were exuberant and lush, the wildflowers purple, yellow and orange, and the grass a brilliant hue. Raising his eyes, he noticed the church on the hillock, the stone cottages huddled around its tall, tapering spire, the cultivated farms, all stripped of life, and wondered: Where are the people of Blake's green and golden land?

The train started with a jerk. He returned to his place and would have tumbled into the lap of a thin, bosomy woman if he had not clutched onto the back of his seat. He apologized politely but the lady looked away. Miffed, Baba cast surreptitious glances at a man seated across from him. He was wearing a shabby knee-length navy blue coat, and grey threadbare shirt; the striped tie was faded and neat. He would have liked to have asked his fellow commuters about the current state of bombed-out London but felt too shy and somewhat invisible; by the time he disembarked at Euston Station his heart was fluttering wildly, like that of a bird blown thousands of miles off course. The passengers hurried away and he felt a touch of envy because they had an address to go to; perhaps friends or relatives had come to receive them.

He waited for the compartment to empty before lowering his cumbersome luggage onto the platform. Except for the occasional drift of conversation from the farther end where soldiers were lounging against kit bags, all was silent. With a nervous flutter he wondered how he would transport his luggage to a taxi. As he was attempting to lift his massive trunk, the trundle of a trolley interrupted his efforts. When his cases were loaded, Baba told the porter that he was an overseas student without any fixed accommodation.

"I'll expect you'll want the Victoria League Hostel, then," the man said.

Grateful for the quick suggestion, he followed the porter out of the station and shivered as the cold air enveloped his head and entered his ears. The sky was still the colour of wood ash, the slate clouds once again low and pregnant with rain. A dull evening had settled on the shadowless streets. Baba hurried into a taxi, grateful for its warmth. He was wrapping the woollen scarf more snugly around his neck when he was afforded the first glimpse of the devastation caused by the Blitz.

Even though he had read the descriptions and seen the photographs, the enormity of the wreckage cut off his breath. Massive, untidy mountains of bricks and mortar lined both sides of a curved street, the skyline made jagged by charred ruins and trembling carcasses of trees. He blinked at the thought of how the street might have appeared to anyone walking down its middle after the bombing, hemmed in by towering walls of fire and billowing smoke. When the driver turned into an untouched part of the neighbourhood, he was struck by how the sight of intact houses ought to have been comforting, but appeared dark and sinister instead, windows papered over by the necessity of war. The front lights of the few cars that were plying the streets had been reduced to slits.

"It doesn't get much worse than this," the driver said, perhaps noticing his passenger fidgeting uneasily in the back.

Baba dropped the fare into the driver's palm in front of the Victoria League. The man drove away, leaving in his wake a forlorn silence.

Inside the front entrance, Baba was told to set his luggage in the corner by the fire extinguisher. When that was done, the concierge walked Baba down the stairs into the lower reaches of the building. For a moment, Baba thought he was being shown into a storage area. But instead, he was led into a very large, dimly lit hall where row upon row of empty beds lined the walls double-decker style, the belongings of occupants stowed haphazardly underneath the lower bunks.

The concierge said, "You'll be comfortable here, alongside the foreign students." The man's tone was condescending and Baba felt a sharp prickle along his scalp.

Upstairs in the dining hall, an unfamiliar odour permeated the air, and the clash of steel cutlery and china sounded stark against the background of muted voices. Baba was given a dinner plate and told to find a place to sit. He sat at the end of an occupied bench and the man seated next to him passed him a sandwich. The sparse white butter was greasy and he could barely taste the jam. But he was starving and there were lots of sandwiches and he helped himself to more when he saw others do so. He refused the soup because there was meat in it. Someone asked him where he was from. "India," he said. Like him, the others were all students, and had travelled from afar. Some were from Jamaica, others from Singapore, East Africa, Tibet.

After dinner, the students helped him carry his luggage to the basement. When it was time to sleep, he removed his nightclothes and changed into them quickly, the dank chill covering his body like a mantle of ice. He glanced at the occupants of the neighbouring beds as they chattered amongst themselves and made an awkward pretence of following their conversation whenever one of them looked his way.

Around ten o'clock someone switched off the lights. Baba lay on his bed and closed his eyes and immediately saw Vasanti, head cocked to one side, staring at an open page of poetry as though it were hieroglyphics. What a fool he had been to leave her. In an attempt to keep warm, he drew up his thighs to his chest; before falling asleep, he resolved to get in touch with Christopher the very next day.

After breakfast the following morning, Baba went to the

ground-floor office and passed to the concierge a piece of paper on which was written his friend's address. The man peered at it and removed from a pigeonhole of his desk a map of London. Baba right away asked where he could purchase one of his own and was told that for reasons of wartime security, maps were not available to the public. Instead, the concierge handed Baba a foolscap paper and dictated very patiently the exact route Baba should take. He reminded Baba to obtain a ration card and gave instructions on how to do so. And before Baba could thank him, he reached down and opened a drawer in a curt act of dismissal.

As he set out for the day, Baba felt marginally better, buoyed by the sun that was showing in a golden curve above a heap of clouds. Across the street, fallen bricks were stowed against the torn outer wall of a public garden in front of which little uniformed children led by older siblings walked to school. Outside the tube station was a table on which was stacked a pile of newspapers alongside a tin. People wishing to buy a copy dropped a few coins into the tin and walked away, the newspaper tucked underneath their arm: Baba stood watching, struck by the honest civility of it all. At the post office he sent off a telegram informing his family that he had arrived.

And now that the time to meet his friend was at hand, he all at once felt reluctant and shy. Not straying too far from the written directions, he nevertheless allowed himself to explore the narrow alleyways and paved lanes, and marvelled at the magnificent stone buildings that lined the streets. And just as a distant clock was chiming the noon hour, he found himself at one of the junctions of five busy avenues. Searching for a place to eat, he spotted a restaurant to his right. He stood inside its entrance and surveyed the room. The few that were seated inside were older gentlemen wearing similar embossed ties; they watched him quite openly, burning ciga-rettes clutched between their fingers. Baba wondered whether he had entered a private club and was just about to leave when a waiter approached. The man led him to a table away from the seated customers, close to a large window. The waiter handed him a menu that contained two choices of meat. Conscious of curious eyes, he explained with a flushed neck that he had only recently arrived from India and that he was a vegetarian. An older gentleman seated across the room nodded imperceptibly and the waiter right away said that he would get him something to eat.

The waiter brought out some soup and bread, and a side dish consisting of two scrawny potatoes and thick pieces of a single boiled carrot. The bread was of a dirty brown but edible, and after making sure that there were no pieces of meat in the soup, Baba tried a spoonful. For pudding Baba was served the only item on the menu: it was semi-sweet, of limited portion and the blancmange texture so novel that he couldn't decide whether he liked it or not. While he ate, he watched two men load their wheelbarrows with debris before tipping the waste into a heap by the side of a collapsed house; he wondered with a shudder how and where London disposed of its wreckage.

~ FOURTEEN ~

ABA KNOCKED ON CHRISTOPHER'S door at three o' clock in the afternoon. A girl, her dark uncombed hair falling to her waist, opened it and said, "I do believe you have the wrong house."

Just as Baba was beginning to think that a door was about to be slammed in his face, the girl opened it wider. "I almost didn't recognize you. It is Vijay, isn't it?" She pronounced it *V-J*. "What on earth are you doing here?"

It was Christopher's sister. "Susan!" he said. "It's been so long since we met."

After shaking Baba's hand enthusiastically, the girl wrapped her baggy cardigan tighter across her body and, stepping to one side, said, "Do come in."

The narrow entrance of the house was dark; thick

blackout material covered the windows. Susan led him into the sitting room and gestured for him to take a seat. "What are you doing here?" she repeated. "When did you arrive?"

"Just yesterday," he answered, then went on to explain the purpose of his visit.

"You chose a fine time to study law!" was all she said, though her tone implied that he must be stupid or mad.

"Christopher is still at work, I take it. I wrote him I was coming and heard back from him but without any mention of my news."

"Your letters probably crossed," Susan said.

Baba started to say he didn't think so, but Susan began to tell him how engineers in the city were always occupied with some repair job or the other, and that on most days Christopher didn't return home until well after dark. She proceeded to list the inconveniences caused by the war, and Baba remembered how she had looked the last time he had seen her: sturdy, with lighter hair, her feet clad in leather sandals, her limbs a deep tanned brown. Now she was pencil-thin and pale, legs covered in stockings under a brown skirt that fell just below her knees.

"I ought to go," he said when she was finished speaking. He moved forward in his seat.

"Don't do that, Vijay, because I know Christopher would never forgive me if I didn't ask you to wait. He missed you a lot, you know, when he first left India. But let me get you a cup of tea. I was just about to make one for myself."

Baba sat back even as she handed him a mass of newspapers, then disappeared into the kitchen. He read about the Nazi occupation of France, the fall of Sevastopol in early July, and Whitehall's reluctance to launch into a concerted invasion of mainland Europe. And all at once, his laudatory image of the unconquerable island nation that ruled almost one-third of the world began to crumble: It was almost three years since the bombs had first fallen, and inexplicable to him why Britain and her Allies had yet to win the war.

Susan returned. "It's all doom and gloom as you can see," she said, placing the wooden tray on a table in front of him. She lifted the teapot. He took the cup from her hand and as he did so a small rumble issued from his stomach.

"It'll take a few days before you get used to the reduced rations," she said, and reached for a tin box that lay on a table next to the sofa. When she opened the lid and removed the butter paper, Baba instantly recognized the naan katai biscuits that his mother used to order for him at Chafékar Wadi.

"They're my favourite," Susan said. "Father sent them out recently in a care package. Help yourself to at least a couple."

He savoured the buttery taste of home and after mopping the crumbs with his forefinger he placed them in his mouth.

Susan set down her cup. "It's my turn to volunteer at the church so I'm afraid I'll have to be on my way. But promise me you will stay here until Christopher returns. Stretch out on the couch if you like. Use that blanket by the fireplace. What with the blackout shades, and the lack of sunshine, it's difficult to tell sometimes whether it is night or day."

He tried to thank her but she cut him off, and after she left, he removed his shoes, shook open the blanket and lay down. There was that silence again, as though every particle in the air was static, without energy or sound. The room was well furnished, with handsome scarlet wallpaper, polished side tables, and plump sofas dressed in striped silk. Paintings, whose details could not be seen in the dimmed light, and portraits of men in army uniform adorned the walls; the large gilded mirror reflected wallpaper covered in turquoise peacocks, and on the side table was a miniature dollhouse. He looked into it, struck by the detail with which the pictures on the walls and the furniture on the floor had been painted and fashioned, the precision with which the tiny members of the family were richly clothed.

His thoughts turned to Vasanti and how much he was missing her; a love letter was gathering momentum inside his head when he heard the sound of a door being opened. Christopher entered the room.

"Bloody hell!" he said, upon seeing Baba on the couch. "Susan must have let you in. Didn't think you'd get here so soon!"

Christopher was holding out his hand and Baba felt a surge of joy even as he shook it. Breaking their hold, Christopher fumbled in his pocket and removed a squashed package of cigarettes; he tapped one out and offered it to Baba.

Baba declined.

Christopher lit his own and said, "Look at you, come all this way in the middle of the war, just for an education. What was the hurry?"

Somewhat put out by his friend's censuring tone, Baba ignored the question. "I didn't think the city would be this wrecked."

"It's insane, is it not? We came pretty close to being hit ourselves. A few hundred yards down the street, a whole row of houses was bombed. The missus of one was away at the time and returned home to find it completely demolished. She still searches the rubble for her two children. She's batty of course. It's a wonder the lot of us aren't."

Christopher continued to take long and frequent drags from his cigarette as he related stories about the horrors of the Blitz, and Baba had a peculiar sense that he was talking to fill what might become an awkward silence.

"It was a pleasant surprise to see Susan," Baba said.

"It's been hard on her. She's never quite settled here, you know; looks upon her time in India as her days of glory."

All at once Baba remembered the circumstances under which Susan had left Nagpur. Twenty or so at the time, she had had a dalliance with an Indian boy—or so the Watson servants had informed the Chafékar servants—that had resulted in her being shipped out to England.

Christopher removed his glasses and wiped them on his trousers. "So, tell me, what are your immediate plans?"

"Registering myself at the Inner Temple, I suppose. I'm keeping my fingers crossed that it is still open to students."

"Very little in London has shut down. Londoners are a dogged lot, you must know. We go about our daily lives as though nothing has happened and perhaps are rewarded for this by a casualty rate that isn't commensurate with the kind of hammering that was inflicted upon us during the Blitz." Christopher got up. "Would you like a cup of tea?"

"I had some with Susan, along with the naan katai biscuits sent by your father." He followed his friend into the kitchen.

When they returned to the sitting room Christopher, a cup of tea in hand, asked Baba how things were with his family.

Baba informed him about his marriage to Vasanti, which he had not mentioned to Christopher in his letters.

His friend listened quietly, and when Baba stopped talking, asked, just as Baba had anticipated, "How could you leave your wife so soon after your marriage?"

Baba had rehearsed an answer. "We'll keep that conversation for another day. But how about you? Have you found someone?"

"I do believe I have."

"When can I meet her?"

Christopher hesitated. "I'll see if she is free some day." He didn't elaborate and Baba did not press him further. "Tell me, though, where are you staying?"

"The Victoria League Hostel." Baba grimaced. "I shall have to look for better accommodation, preferably near the Inns of Court. But until then, is it all right if I stayed here with you?"

"This house doesn't belong to us," Christopher said. "It belongs to Nigel, Mother's cousin. He's stationed in Africa and only too happy to have the property looked after."

Feeling stung by Christopher's reluctance to help, Baba watched his friend light another cigarette. He took in Christopher's blackened nails, the tousled hair, the unshaven jaw, the deep gash between his eyebrows, and concluded that it was most likely the war and its attending stresses that were now putting a strain on their friendship.

"I'd better go," he said, and stood up reluctantly, not at all happy at the thought of stepping into the cold.

Christopher walked him to the door.

"I have a little something for you. Vasanti, my wife, helped me pick it out."

"She shouldn't have gone to all that trouble."

"Do you have a telephone?" Baba asked.

"We do, but it's not working."

"I'll bring over the parcel after I've found somewhere to stay."

"You do that," Christopher said, and stifled a yawn as he shut the door.

Christopher's cool response agitating his thoughts, Baba fell asleep that night listening to the students toss and turn around him. In the morning he set out to obtain a ration card, and after presenting the relevant papers, was surprised by the efficiency with which his request was met. He decided to walk to the Inner Temple since it wasn't far. Once again, he was confronted by a low sky, dull pavement and the uneven sight of enemy action juxtaposed with undamaged brick buildings darkened by the effluence of coal.

By the time he reached his destination it was pelting rain. He looked around for assistance, but not a person was within sight. When he finally came upon the offices of the Inner Temple they were barred and a notice on the door said that they would remain unmanned until the twenty-fourth of

August on account of repairs. That was four weeks away. Feeling wretchedly thwarted, he wished he had never left India. It was afternoon in Nagpur now and Vasanti and his sisters-in-law were most likely sitting in the shaded part of the veranda, drinking tea accompanied by savoury snacks. Failing to block out other memories of Vasanti, he scoured the neighbourhood for a TO LET sign, and saw one in the front window of a house that appeared to be suitable, its front garden well tended and neat. He noted down its address.

At the hostel he entered the empty basement and climbed onto his bunk bed, silence drilling holes into his eardrums, hunger giving him stomach cramps. And after yet another meagre and unsatisfactory meal, he donned his raincoat, and headed to the house with the room to let. He walked up the front path bordered by lavender bushes and rang the doorbell. A woman stuck out her head and asked Baba what he would be wanting. He pointed to the sign in the window and said he was looking for lodging. She asked him to step in, and introduced herself as Mrs. Pinter. She wore large round spectacles with steel frames; a flowery apron covered her stooping torso.

"My name is Vijay Chafékar," Baba said. "I'm a student from India."

He started to remove his shoes.

"You can leave them on," she said.

She led him into a basement kitchen where her husband was seated. He shook Baba's hand and without a word went back to fixing a small wooden box with hinges that had become undone.

There were plates on the wall and little copper moulds. The water pipes gurgled erratically and a light drizzle was trickling down the windowpane. Mrs. Pinter offered Baba a place by the stove, from which a very small heat was emanating. She asked him informal questions related to the purpose of his London visit and the length of his stay, then sat back in her chair. After a few minutes she quoted the price of the room and enquired whether he was still interested in seeing it. He nodded and followed her up the stairs. On the third floor landing, when the light from the hallway gave way to sudden darkness, she lit a candle that had been standing in a jar on the step.

She led him down a short passage and pushed open a door. A musty smell emerged.

He followed her in, and as she walked him around its periphery, holding out the candle towards the corners, Baba noted that except for a bed, cupboard, and desk with a chair, the room was uncarpeted and bare. The curtains on the window were of a heavy, yellow material.

"The bathroom and lavatory are on the second floor. You will share them with us and two other boarders."

"That suits me fine," Baba quickly said, thinking that a private room with shared facilities was still a better option than the dormitory at the Victoria League Hostel.

Mrs. Pinter led him back down the stairs. "I think we have another boarder," she announced to her husband.

Mr. Pinter looked up at Baba and bade him a pleasant welcome. Baba returned his smile and asked Mrs. Pinter whether he could move in the following day.

"There are there no dietary restrictions, are there?" she asked.

"I'm vegetarian," Baba said.

"I've never served a vegetarian before." Mrs. Pinter looked at her husband.

"He can always eat in a restaurant, I suppose," Mr. Pinter said.

"I don't mind serving the odd vegetarian meal," Mrs. Pinter conceded. "I could give you bread and tea for breakfast. But for something more substantial, you might want to try the communal canteens where meals are supplied at cost."

"You don't want to be taking money for those meals," Mr. Pinter reminded his wife.

"Of course not," she replied. "I'll discount lunch and supper from the rent."

They shook hands at the front door and Baba slipped away, his mind anxious at the thought of the smallness of the house and the meagre furnishings of his room. And as he took long strides he found himself thinking how he would not be describing to Vasanti his living quarters.

The following late afternoon, he retraced his steps to his friend, his eagerness to tell Christopher about his success in finding accommodation overriding the awkwardness of their previous encounter.

He rang the doorbell, his parcel for Christopher held out in front of him. This time a different girl opened the door.

A bit flustered, he lowered his hands and asked whether Christopher was in.

"And who shall I say is calling?" The girl's voice was unfriendly, almost suspicious.

Before he could reply, his friend came forward and, wrapping his arm around the girl's shoulder, quickly said, "Isobel, this is Vijay."

Isobel nodded curtly and stepped back. His cheeks and neck mottled bright red, Christopher gestured for Baba to enter. The house was colder than he remembered it and there was a cloying scent in the air. He followed his hosts into the sitting room. There was no sign of Susan.

"She left early today—Susan, that is," Christopher said, reading Baba's mind just the way he used to at Chafékar Wadi.

Baba handed Christopher the present that Vasanti had so carefully wrapped. His friend smiled and laid it on the coffee table.

"Aren't you going to open it?" Baba asked.

"Shall I?"

"Of course," Baba said.

"Do sit down," Christopher said. He pulled on the ribbon, unwrapping with care, and explained to Isobel the purpose of Baba's visit to London, adding that he had known Baba since his Nagpur days.

Isobel did not reply. She patted and pushed her hair into place; it was brown and fell to her shoulders. Her forehead was covered in curls and small earrings clipped her earlobes.

"Look, Isobel," Christopher said with a happy smile, holding up a silk shirt that was a soft, luminous yellow. He picked up the contrasting scarlet tie embossed with black paisleys and held it against the shirt.

Delighted by his friend's response, Baba pointed to the gift box. "Isn't there something else?"

Christopher rummaged inside and held up a package of sugared almonds. "You must taste them, Isobel," he said. "Vijay's mother would—"

"How quickly he forgets," Isobel addressed Baba, "that nuts don't suit me."

Turning away and trying to ignore her petulance, Baba informed Christopher about his unsuccessful visit to the Inns of Court, and of his success at finding suitable lodgings, adding that he would like to invite Christopher—and Isobel of course—to his new digs for a cup of tea.

Christopher said, "Did you clear that with your landlady?"

"Clear what?"

"Not all rooming houses allow visitors."

Baba was taken aback.

Isobel said, "You are not in India, you know. It's years since Christopher left Nagpur but every now and then I have occasion to remind him that he is back home now and must think and feel as a British person."

There was a brief pause, during which Christopher did not offer Baba refreshments but muttered something inane about the weather.

Enunciating slowly, Isobel asked Baba just how much longer he was expecting to stay in London.

"I think getting admitted to the bar is at most a two-year process—the fact is, I won't know until I've spoken to the Registrar."

"I rather thought you might have found out before venturing out this far." She gave a little sniff.

Realizing that he'd made a poor impression on Isobel, Baba stood up abruptly and the ridiculous cap that covered the armrest of the sofa fell to the carpet. He picked it up. Christopher said in his most apologetic voice, "Don't bother." But they both knew that it was too late; that the moment for signalling to Isobel the true nature of their friendship had long since passed.

Back in Nagpur, if Vasanti had behaved like this, Baba might have said, "Christopher is a dear childhood friend and the longer he stays in Nagpur the better I will like it."

But they were not in India and Isobel wasn't Vasanti. Placing the cap on the armrest, Baba asked Christopher to convey his regards to Susan. Isobel walked to the front door ahead of them and opened it. Christopher held out his hand, thanked Baba for the gift with genuine gratitude. The door clicked shut after him even before Baba was back on the sidewalk.

Engulfed by humiliation, Baba was hard-pressed to understand why Christopher had allowed Isobel's response to get in the way of their friendship? Would she not have felt better disposed towards him if Christopher had told her—just the way Baba had told Vasanti—about their closeness? So, why hadn't he? For the second time within a nine-month span he felt shamefully betrayed. First his father, and to a certain extent his brothers, and now his best friend—each had let him down in an unexpected way.

Baba removed his raincoat, and kept walking, telling himself that he *would not, must not* get in touch with Christopher anytime soon. Maybe later, somewhere in October or November, when he was well settled and had a good sense of his academic plans, maybe then he would visit him once again. But it was difficult for him to dismiss Christopher from his life or his thoughts. When he had resolved to leave India, the unpleasant circumstances of that decision and, later, the pain and remorse had largely been mitigated by the fact that he would get to see and spend time with his old friend again. Little had he dreamt that Christopher would be a changed person, one who had different priorities now.

The previous time Baba had sought out Christopher, he had walked past The Red Lion and a glimpse inside had told him that it was cozy and quaint. Shaking with guilt, he entered it now and stood in front of the bar, his eyes grazing the row upon row of upside-down bottles reflected in the mirror. He ordered a Guinness, the very first recognizable bottle his eyes fell upon. He took the dark drink and sat in a wooden chair, his back turned to a group of men and women talking rapidly in nasal tones, the occasional laugh-aloud exhortation causing him to dart a quick glance to see whether their laughter was about him. His sense of alienation and his shame at having partaken of an alcoholic drink increasing, he nevertheless drained his glass and quickly consumed a second before leaving the pub.

The overcast afternoon had turned into a clear evening. Baba returned to the hostel and with the help of a couple of students left his belongings next to the fire extinguisher on the main floor. Afterwards, he went to the dining hall for supper, and by the time he got up from the table, the weighty, disaffected feeling was replaced by a congenial glow: the Guinness had hit its mark.

~ FIFTEEN ~

BABA TOOK A TAXI TO MRS. PINTER and deposited his luggage in the narrow front lobby. The two other boarders helped him carry it up to his attic room. Paul Hewitt, a pale man with thin arms and legs, appeared to be in his thirties. Mr. Hudson, with his creased brow and prominent Adam's apple, seemed a little older.

Later that night, thinking of Vasanti and surrounded by bare necessities, Baba resolved to fast-track his journey to get admitted to the bar. Christopher had once told him that keeping terms at the Inner Temple was relatively easy, and even if it wasn't, Baba was willing to study around the clock if it meant he could return to Vasanti that much sooner.

He drifted off to sleep. And when he awakened, he lay a while, fighting the urge to remain underneath the blankets, inside the warmth. He got dressed and went downstairs quietly, so as not to disturb the sleeping occupants, clutching in one hand a large paper bag containing some edibles. The kitchen echoed with the loud ticking of a wall clock. He looked at it and gave a start. It was almost noon.

He was standing at the narrow basement window when he heard the front door open and close. Soon Mrs. Pinter came downstairs.

"There are strict mealtimes in this lodging house," she said, her tone disapproving.

"I'm sorry. I have yet to unpack my alarm clock," Baba explained, taken aback. He held out the two-pound package filled with tea leaves he had brought from Nagpur and a large bag of dried fruit.

"For you," he said. "That is, for everyone who lives here." She thanked him with a surprised smile and put some water on to boil.

"What's that?" she asked, pointing to an envelope on the table.

"A month's rent, in advance."

She looked pleased, but left the envelope lying there and busied herself with lunch.

He had to pick up his courage to ask, "I have a friend here . . . that is, is it possible to have him and his sister come over for a cup of tea one day?" He had decided not to include Isobel in that first invitation.

"I'm afraid that won't be possible. There are three lodgers, and if each of you brought in visitors—well, I'm afraid I cannot make an exception just for you."

"That's all right," Baba said quickly, even as the notion that he would have to look for somewhere else to live entered his head.

Perhaps to compensate for her inflexibility, and even though she had said that he would have to get his lunch and dinner at a communal canteen, Mrs. Pinter placed in front of him two thick slices of bread and a pot of tea.

"When do you expect to begin your studies at the Inns of Court?" she asked.

"I don't know as yet. I went there yesterday to make inquiries, but the office is closed until the third week of August."

"So what will you do in the meantime?"

"Well . . . I thought I might travel outside London for a bit," Baba said, seized by a sudden longing to escape this inhospitable house. "Do you have any suggestions for where I could go?"

Mrs. Pinter thought for a while. "Every summer—that is, before the war—we would holiday in North Wales. In a place called Harlech. It's very beautiful up there."

"You think I might like it?"

"Harlech has stretches of beautiful beach, but there wouldn't be much for you to do, except maybe explore the castle. If you want something vigorous, however, you might try climbing Mount Snowdon, which is also in North Wales. Not all the way to the top, of course. It's much too demanding an ascent to go it alone. But even if you were to climb for a bit, the views are rewarding."

After lunch, Baba followed Mrs. Pinter up the stairs and retrieved his raincoat and scarf. Thrusting open his umbrella, he stepped into the drizzle, side-stepping puddles with optimism now that his dilemma of how to congenially pass some of the ensuing weeks was solved.

In spite of the rain, it was warmer outside. He loosened the uppermost button of his raincoat and went in search of a post office, and when he returned, tucked away inside his jacket was an aerogram for the letter to Vasanti that he intended to write. He opened the door of his lodging with the key he had been given by Mrs. Pinter, only to be greeted by the unfamiliar stillness of an empty house.

He was standing at the front window when he saw his landlady walking down the lane, carrying packages in her hands. He opened the door. They went downstairs to the kitchen and he watched as Mrs. Pinter stacked the provisions on the shelves.

When she finished, Baba passed her his small diary. "I wrote a letter while you were out. I wish to send my family my return address. Would you write it out for me, please?"

Mrs. Pinter picked up a pen and said, "I don't know at all whether this is true. There are all kinds of rumours these days. But they do say that letters posted outside London are sorted quicker and reach their destination earlier than those sent from the city. Since you are leaving London, you may want to post your letter elsewhere."

Armed with directions from Mrs. Pinter, Baba set out for North Wales very early the following day. This time, his train compartment was filled with young, chattering ladies dressed in smart uniform, and the five hours it took to reach Chester were spent in a pleasant fashion even as he tried to discern their unfamiliar accents. He stayed the night in a hotel, and the following morning, sunshine fuelling his sense of well-being, caught a bus to Llanberis, a packed lunch and a tall flask of tea added to his luggage.

By the time he began his ascent of Mount Snowdon, the day was half over, but had nevertheless retained its warmth. He climbed for a while, noticing that the railway line Mrs. Pinter had mentioned was sometimes to his left, other times to his right. From the odd chimney deep in the valley an ascending string of smoke was getting smudged in the wind-swept sky. He continued to climb for half an hour; the path became steeper and more rugged, and since he was carrying in his hand a heavy clutch bag filled with a week's clothing, he thought he would conceal it behind a bush. He marked the spot by making a high mound of the rocks that were scattered on the hillside, and after returning to the path he ate his lunch, a distinctive ridge formed by three mountains to his left, the valley at their base dotted with crumbling farms.

He resumed his climb and made steady progress, and it wasn't until quite some time later that he noticed the wind was beginning to pick up and the air was turning chilly. Thrusting his hands into his pockets, he paused to enjoy the view. Shadows were drifting across the landscape, loose clouds were grazing the sun. Still, it was mostly clear, and as he made his way up, all he could think about was how one day he would bring Vasanti to North Wales and point out to her the woolly sheep, the reflecting lakes, the staff-carrying shepherd boys, the lush valleys juxtaposed with the bare and rocky summit of Mount Snowdon.

His laboured breathing the only sound in the engulfing silence, he moved higher, stumbling up a steep, scraggy slope. The path was slippery now and it was imperative to watch his step. When next he came to a level outcrop and lifted his head, he noticed that a thick fog was descending, and before he could resolve whether to flee down the mountain or stay where he was, it bound him in its opaque grip. He could barely make out a boulder and sat on it, a little frightened because he had never before experienced such swift inclemency. He calmed himself with the thought that just as suddenly as it had taken a turn for the worse, the weather would no doubt get better.

As he sat huddled, his legs braced against the wet cold, he considered everything that had happened to him in the previous nine months. He knew now that his obdurate resolution to come here, alone and in the midst of a war, had been a grave mistake. Even as he was thinking that there was no escaping the loneliness of the following months, he remembered what Vasanti's cousin had advised him at the Bombay docks: that Baba should return to India if things did not work out for him in any way.

Vasanti, he knew, was missing him as much as he missed her. Baba wished that he could have brought her with him to England. Yet it was difficult to picture her happy in this cold, lonely place, isolated from everything and everyone that she knew and loved so well.

His thoughts turned to his father, and Baba contemplated yet again the man Nanasahib had chosen to spend his life with. The questions Baba had assiduously avoided during his three-week voyage to Liverpool now returned. Ramabai had stoically accepted Nanasahib's unusual relationship, so why was it that he, the son closest to his mother, had not imbibed her tolerant and forgiving attitude when his own brothers had taken her cue and made peace with Nanasahib? Was it not they who had continued to give him the respect due to a father, and consequently saved the family from fracture and harm? If his own brothers had learned to live with the truth, however bizarre and shocking it might be, what had prevented him from making a similar choice? The answers to these painful questions eluded him, and the unresolved conflict made him feel frustrated, petty-minded, weak.

The cold was perishing now. Standing up, he untied the thick pullover that he had knotted around his waist. He unbuttoned his raincoat and let it drop, in a hurry to get the bulky jumper over his head; and when he reached down to retrieve it, it wasn't there. Thinking it must have fallen behind the boulder, he knelt and peered over its edge. His heart all but stopped: the boulder was perched on the verge of a steep drop and in the fog he could discern the smudge of his coat halfway down the slope, nestled inside a bush. The inner pocket contained his passport and his diary together with the letter he had written Vasanti. He had no choice but to retrieve it.

He lowered himself next to the boulder and, testing the slippery terrain with his feet, began to slide gradually forward, his eyes locked on the raincoat some thirty feet below. He was making good progress descending the slope on his backside when his foot began to glide and in that frightening, uncertain moment, he clutched the gnarled trunk of a dwarf tree and hauled himself once again into a sitting position.

Taking care, he moved onward, and when he was within arms' length of the coat, he leaned forward to grab it . . . but before his hand could make contact, he found himself once again thrown off balance. He reached out both arms this time but there was no thicket or tree he could hang onto, only slick, wet moss, and before he could sit upright his body began to accelerate, and just before he turned onto his stomach in an attempt to brake his slide, the back of his head hit something sharp, and his world was plunged into darkness.

III

August to October 1942

LONDON AND NORTH WALES, UK

~ SIXTEEN ~

SITTING IN THE breakfast room of The London Gate Hotel, his recovered memory sending relief through his body, Baba gazes at the pots of frangipani massed at the entrance to the dining hall and addresses a thanksgiving prayer to Lord Shiva for restoring to him his beloved Vasanti. His mind expanding with warm gratitude, he thanks the Lord yet again for Mr. Owens, for his unquestioning and generous hospitality, without which Baba, alone and hopeless, might still be trying to find his past. Then the tainted memory of Catherine pushes forward and all but drains his gratefulness. The dreaded remembrance of what took place in the stone shelter is subsumed by the shocking realization of what his adultery will mean to Vasanti. But what if he were not to tell her anything? She will be none the wiser, and he will justifiably bear the whole burden of his guilt. He remembers the accusation he had made against his father, about how disloyal Nanasahib had been to Ramabai, and feels ashamed now at having committed a transgression similar to the one that had so repulsed him.

He dips his knife into his half-congealed egg and drinks several cups of tea to quench his thirst. Afterwards he goes upstairs to his room, on his way picking up a sprig of frangipani that has broken off its stem and tumbled to the carpet.

Later that morning, he checks out of his hotel and hails a taxi to his former lodgings. With forced composure, he rings Mrs. Pinter's doorbell.

Her pale face beaming with relief, Mrs. Pinter calls out to her husband that Mr. Vijay has returned. Mr. Pinter hurries up from the kitchen and he, too, greets Baba with surprised pleasure.

Baba is gladdened by their smiles. In the sitting room he removes his cap and settles into the offered chair. Mr. Pinter says that he will make them all cups of tea. When he returns with the teapot, Mrs. Pinter says to Baba, "Dare I confess that I'd given up hope of seeing you, so worried was I that something bad had happened? I thought you would return to London within three or four days, a week at the most. There's only so much one can see and do in North Wales."

"I would have sent you a message had I been able," Baba says. "I took a very bad fall on Mount Snowdon and ended up losing my memory. It has taken me this long to find it." His voice is guarded.

"I'm so sorry to hear that," Mrs. Pinter says, glancing at her husband, her eyes round with surprise. Nevertheless, she does not press him for details and Baba is grateful for her reserve.

As they eat biscuits and sip hot tea, Mrs. Pinter says, "You look worn out. I expect it'll take you a few days to recover from your ordeal."

"Yes," Baba says. "It is Friday today and the Inner Temple offices are closed for repairs until Monday. So I think I'll rest until then."

As planned, Baba keeps to his room during the week-end, walking down to the basement kitchen only to consume for breakfast, lunch and supper the invariable bread, butter and tea. Ashamed of his recent dietary lapse, he does not tell Mrs. Pinter that during his amnesia he developed a taste and appetite for non-vegetarian food. Back in his room he opens his trunk and unpacks some of his belongings. Although he has decided that he must soon move to more comfortable lodgings, he feels too discouraged by all that has happened to search for better accommodation right away. He starts to write another letter to Vasanti, one that might replace the letter lost at the bottom of a cliff on

Mount Snowdon, but the appalling thought of his infidelity keeps him from finishing it. Instead he distracts himself by completing a short communication to his father informing him that all is well, omitting altogether any mention of his excursion to North Wales. His identity restored, he sleeps undisturbed and at length.

By Monday morning, Baba is ready to leave the house. He takes a taxi to the Inner Temple. Its offices are open. He hands his academic transcripts along with the college's letter of acceptance to an official named Mr. Robinson, who is manning the desk.

The gentleman is impressed that Baba has travelled all the way from India to be admitted to the bar. "I commend you for not allowing the war to disrupt your plans," he says. "As my father always used to say, 'Whatever happens, you just have to get on with it.'"

His immediate paperwork completed, Baba mentions to Mr. Robinson that he had come by the office at the beginning of the month and found that the college offices were closed.

"Yes, considerable damage was sustained by the Inner Temple," Mr. Robinson acknowledges. "In May last year, the Temple Church was destroyed. All that remains standing are the outer walls and the vaulting. And even earlier, in September of the previous year, an explosive bomb sliced open the Library clock tower."

Baba is taken aback. "Is it possible for me to see the church and the library?"

"Yes, of course." Mr. Robinson accompanies Baba to the door and points out the direction he should take. "Don't forget to submit the two letters of recommendation," he adds.

Baba makes his way to the bombed-out site. Viewing the destruction, he is struck by the frightening notion that had he been studying in the library when the bombs had fallen, thousands of crashing books and crumbling stonewalls would have buried him alive. A hollow sensation spreading inside his gut, he hastily turns away.

Less than two weeks remain until the start of term. Baba sets about contacting a couple of barristers whose names have been given to him by Nanasahib and is grateful when both are amenable to certifying to the Inner Temple that Baba is a respectable gentleman, worthy of enrollment. This stipulation met, he turns his attention to the remaining two conditions spelled out by Mr. Robinson: he is required to keep twelve terms, and must pass all his examinations before being formally called to the bar. In addition, there is an expectation that he will eat six out of every twenty-four suppers served each term, in the Inner Temple dining hall. Finding nothing difficult about these requirements, he purchases his textbooks and lines them up on his desk in the attic room at Mrs. Pinter's. He checks his wardrobe to make sure he has sufficient warm clothing, and is pleased to discover that he has.

He removes from his desk an extra package of dried fruit and for lack of a bowl pours out a handful onto his palm. His stomach feels hollow most of the time now, and he finds himself sometimes waking in the middle of the night with hunger cramps. He has begun taking his lunch and supper at a neighbouring restaurant, and although tempted by the beef and roast lamb—but not at all by the liver sausages—written in chalk on the menu board, he stoically confines himself to all that is vegetarian.

It is a warm, humid morning when Baba begins his classes. The first week passes quickly, and he is relieved to note that the academic work is not taxing. He makes comfortable inroads into Roman Law and Common Law, and finds himself purchasing cramming notes, which are easily available and have been recommended to him by other students, as adequate preparation for exams.

Increasingly, even as he reads his law books and notes late into the night, three thoughts assume permanent shape inside his head: a deep-seated intuition that tells him leaving Vasanti was wrong on all counts; a boundless sense of gratitude towards Mr. Owens for rescuing him; and a sensation of horrified aversion towards what took place in the stone

shed with Catherine. The unmentionable occurrence continues to prevent him from writing to Vasanti. He compensates
for this lack of communication by sending weekly notes to
his father saying that his studies are going along the desired
path. His letters are formal and to the point, and because he
is still keen on finding better accommodation, he furnishes
as his contact address the post office near the Inns of Court.

His evenings are lonely. One of the barristers who
agreed to sponsor him said that he would like to have Baba
over to his home for a meal some time. As the weeks pass,
Baba waits for an invitation, but it does not arrive. The
compulsory suppers at the Inner Temple are intended to
forge a feeling of collegial conviviality and offer an opportunity to make valuable contacts. But Baba finds himself
unable to drum up the energy or the will to carry on an
animated and interested conversation with the other three
seated at his table. They are older students, and the social
exchanges amongst the diners—perhaps because of the
war—are muted and restrained.

Almost every afternoon after class, Baba is drawn to
retrace his footsteps to the partially destroyed library, and
each time his mind is benumbed by the extent of the devastation visited upon London. Sometimes, when the city is
veiled in blackout, when searchlights and volunteer citizens
on terraces comb the sky for enemy activity and vigilant
night wardens make the rounds of the city streets, he joins

the lively crowds inside the cinema halls. Having been enthralled by the James Hilton novel upon which the film is based, he watches *Goodbye Mr. Chips* four times. Every time, he exits the theatre in tears, the dying words of Mr. Chips, or "Chipping," the aged teacher and former headmaster of a boarding school, resonating in his mind: "I thought I heard you saying it was a pity . . . a pity I never had any children. But you're wrong. I have. Thousands of them . . . and all boys." And in spite of the estrangement between them, Baba's heart longs for Nanasahib. He thinks about his brothers, too, and homesickness keeps him awake late into the night.

As a cold and dry autumn sets in, the warmth of summer slowly becomes a distant memory. Baba often walks Oxford Street, which is always thronged with people, and over time he strikes up a nodding friendship with a Persian Muslim family who run a narrow shop that sells everything from fresh produce to candles. Once, they invite him in and insist that he share their barbari flatbread delicately flavoured with sesame seeds. Their smiling hospitality reminds Baba of home. He ducks his head under the awning and joins them in the tiny back room, grateful to be spared even for one meal the taste of the brown bread that is the staple of all London canteens and restaurants. The only other menu items he can eat are the Woolton salad, composed of greens and fresh vegetables; rolls, butter and cheese; ice cream, lemon sponge and rice pudding. Sometimes, the blandness of the food, stripped of all spices and aromatics, causes his stomach to turn, and he skips meals, acutely aware that he is slowly starving himself. Mrs. Pinter always offers him an extra slice at breakfast but he doesn't take it, knowing that he must act like other Londoners and contribute to the war effort the best way he can.

Breakfast times are usually quiet. All he has learned from Paul Hewitt, one of the other boarders, is that Paul is a proud member of the Home Guard, the organization that comprises thousands of local volunteers who are otherwise ineligible for military service. It is a secondary defence force, Mr. Hewitt explains to Baba, in case the forces of Nazi Germany invade London. Mr. Hudson, the third boarder, occasionally brings in flowers from the vegetable and flower gardens he helps maintain around the city. Baba thinks of him every time he passes a plot of land that has been culti-vated into a vegetable patch. One morning, after Mr. Hudson has received a letter from his sister in Alberta, he talks at length about the two very agreeable years he spent on the Canadian prairies when he was a young lad. Even after all this time, Mr. Hudson tells them, he sometimes dreams that he is back in the splendid Rocky Mountains, sitting outside a tent under stars, watching the northern lights sway with the breeze. Urged on by Mrs. Pinter, he talks about the immeasurable blue sky filled with dissimilar cloud formations and varying weather systems; the lush grasslands housing enormous ranches of sheep, cattle, and the free roaming wild horses that travel the country and are a marvel to behold. Mr. Hudson's depiction fascinates Baba and lodges permanently in his imagination.

His disappointment in Christopher having lessened with time, and because of the head trauma he has experienced in Wales, Baba is tempted to get back in touch with his friend and with Susan, but decides to postpone contacting them until he has found a better place to room and board. And so, feeling like an outsider with no real friends to talk to, his loneliness increases by the day. He draws up an eighteen-month calendar of the weeks left until he might finish his studies and return home, and is dismayed to find the days are passing slowly.

One morning, after counting the number of different army uniforms he is able to spot in Trafalgar Square— fifteen—Baba wanders into the National Gallery and finds accomplished musicians warming up their instruments. Realizing he has stumbled into a concert, he takes a seat and stays until the end of the recital. The sublime memory of professional musicians playing classical music lingers with him for days. Once again he is inspired to start a letter to Vasanti but is unable to sustain or finish it. He wants to tell her, for example, about the abundance of women in London who work outside their homes. Across from his lodging is a communal nursery, and when Baba is leaving for his classes in the morning he sees young mothers dressed in uniform dropping off their children for the day. There are other things he wants to tell Vasanti: about the massive barrage balloons in the sky that resemble airborne whales; the fast-flowing Thames choked with river traffic; the beautiful blossoms on flowering trees whose names he does not know; King George VI, barely discernable in the distance, taking a salute from the army as it wends its way in front of Buckingham Palace; the thrilling sight from the rooftop of the first American troops marching in step through the city streets. He visualizes himself back at Chafékar Wadi telling Vasanti all of this and the worm of this thought begins—even before he knows it—to burrow into his mind.

Another communication Baba knows he should not postpone is the thank-you note that Mr. Owens so richly deserves. Classes finished early one late September morning, he walks out of the college determined to return to his lodging and write the letter that very afternoon. But first, as always, he is compelled to make his daily visit to the damaged library. Just as he arrives, two ravens fly up from its ruins, and after calling out to each other in riotous tones are joined by countless others who flex their wings before taking perch. At once repelled and chilled by the image of predatory birds scavenging amongst the rubble, a premonition sweeps through him: the worst is not over, not by far, and he should return to Nagpur without losing another day. The ominous feeling catches him by surprise. Back at Chafékar Wadi when he had told Vasanti that she was not to worry for his safety and that nothing bad was going to happen to him, he had not merely been trying to console her. He had truly believed that nothing untoward would take place. Losing his mother at an early age and having to deal with his father's secret, he figured, was enough retribution and punishment for one existence, adequate to atone for all the misdeeds of his past lives. Yet, how misguided was this supposition—for here he is, only recently having come through the ordeal of losing his memory, of falling ill in the process, of being seduced by Catherine, and now having to suffer through a two-year residence in a city despoiled by war.

Only that morning, Mr. Pinter informed them at the breakfast table of the strong rumour that the Nazis are developing a revenge bomb. If this is true, Baba reasons, the prominent buildings will continue to remain prime targets, and it is likely that the very thing he came to London to achieve will be denied him. For all his recent misfortune, he has been lucky twice: when he made the sea crossing unscathed, and when he recovered his memory without apparent damage to his mind. Other than the permanent loss of those twenty or so hours after he fell and before he was rescued by Mr. Owens, his memory has remained intact. Yet, what guarantee that he will be so lucky the next time? He forces himself to admit the unspeakable: that the only reason he left India was to wound and punish his father by making him suffer, just as Baba had suffered when Nanasahib had caused him to lose faith in the integrity of the parent he had once hero-worshipped. Now, in the light of day, facing the broken state of London, the courage and valour of its loyal, persevering citizens, and the bombed-out ruins before him, the anger he feels towards Nanasahib, the sense of betrayal, the shame, all seem muted, petty and one-dimensional.

His resolve to write his letter to Mr. Owens swept away again by more pressing concerns, Baba continues his walk around the city. He goes to the bank with which Nanasahib has made arrangements, and cashes a cheque that has arrived for him there. It is late afternoon when he makes his way back to his lodging house, tired but flushed with new resolve. He lies on his attic bed and contemplates the measures he will employ to bring about his latest decision: to leave England for home. This time, he is certain that his decision is based not on dashed expectations and self-indulgent emotions but on personal experience and a newfound understanding and sense of responsibility towards his family and his life.

The following day, he informs the college about his decision. And two months after he first set foot in England, Baba again loads his luggage into a taxi, this time for his return journey.

Mrs. Pinter accompanies him outside. "I suppose you can always come back later," she says, "at a better time, when the war is over and life has returned to normal."

"That's always a possibility," Baba concedes.

~ SEVENTEEN ~

AFTER RIDING THE TRAIN to Liverpool Station, Baba stores his belongings for a small fee and catches a bus to the docks. He makes his way to the ticketing office, and informs the man behind the counter that he is a civilian looking to reserve a berth to Bombay.

"You wish to travel to India?"

Having anticipated the incredulity with which his request might be met, Baba explains—as he previously did to Mr. Robinson at the Inner Temple—that he's been called to the bedside of a sick relative. He thinks of this as a white lie; various members of his family are probably filled with anxiety for his safety, and Vasanti no doubt feels lonely and bereft.

The man at the counter disappears into an inner room, returns with a notice and shows it to Baba: *Eastern Star*

TRAVELLING TO SINGAPORE VIA BOMBAY. ESTIMATED
DATE OF DEPARTURE: OCTOBER 30, 1942.

"But that's almost four weeks away!"

The man says nothing, simply lets go of the paper as it
settles on the counter in front of him.

"Well, is there a berth available for me?" Baba asks.

"Most likely you will be bunking down with troops. I
suggest you check in with us a few days before the ship sets
sail. You'll pay at that time, not before."

Crushed, Baba makes his way back to the railway station, cursing the fact that once again he will have to seek
accommodation and find a way to pass his time; there is no
point in returning to London. After he has retrieved his
belongings, he catches a taxi and checks into a nearby hotel.

The first few days pass slowly. Baba walks around war-
damaged Liverpool, eats in small cafés and teashops, borrows
books from the public library and finishes reading *Middlemarch*.
He sees films whose titles he right away forgets, so distracted
is he, and eager to return home. Vasanti is constantly in his
thoughts and when he glimpses girls who resemble her in
deportment and hairstyle, he feels compelled against all reason
to overtake them, to see whether their faces carry any hint of
hers. He has decided not to inform his family about his imminent sea voyage. Doing so would entail providing explana-
tions, which he would rather convey in person. He can't wait
to see their expressions, especially Vasanti's, when he arrives

at Chafékar Wadi unannounced. So that they will not worry about him, he mails a brief note to Nanasahib saying that he is fine, and thanks him for the bank remittance.

One evening towards the end of that first week of October, he is eating supper in the hotel dining room, wondering what he will do until bedtime, when he notices on the sideboard next to him some embossed stationery. His long-held and too-often postponed intention to write to Mr. Owens returns. Knowing that he should not wait a minute longer, he removes a pen from his inner pocket and begins to write. Much as he wishes to block out the existence of Catherine and his adultery, he knows he has been remiss about not conveying the good news of his recovery. Baba informs Mr. Owens of the basic facts: that he arrived in England as a student but is now making his way back to India, perhaps to return at a later date to be admitted to the bar. He thanks his benefactor for looking after him so well and hopes that Catherine is feeling better. He assures the old man that he will send her medicine as soon as he has obtained it. He signs off, wishing them both his very best.

A few days later, Baba is handed at the front desk correspondence addressed to him. It is from North Wales. Mr. Owens expresses delight that his charming amnesiac Hari—he can never think of him as having any other name—has regained his memory, and wishes that he had revealed more about himself in his brief note. Catherine continues to have mixed days, Mr. Owens writes, but does not expand on this. He ends with a sincere invitation, a characteristically hospitable entreaty that Baba visit him and Catherine in North Wales before sailing out on the *Eastern Star*.

Baba is touched by the affectionate letter but tries to put it out of his mind. Nevertheless, over the following day, walking the streets that have become tediously familiar, his thoughts return to Mr. Owens' invitation to visit him. He contemplates the crucial role the old man played, and recognizes that thanking him in person would be the gentlemanly thing to do. Additionally, the thought that he ought to make a confession and apologize about what happened between him and Catherine before leaving for Llandudno Junction continues to haunt him. Keeping her father in the dark, he thinks, is betraying the trust that Mr. Owens continues to place in him. Taking up his invitation to visit will provide the opportunity Baba needs to once and for all thank his benefactor and set his conscience at rest. Remembering the modest cottage and its singular lack of possessions, Baba feels he ought to return the old man's belongings. He makes up his mind: he will visit Mr. Owens during the morning hours when Catherine is sure to be at the day nursery. That way, he will avoid meeting her. He will spend a couple of hours at the cottage and afterwards drive on to Harlech, and spend two days at a seaside hotel, an excursion originally recommended by Mrs. Pinter.

Having made his decision, Baba rents a car from an elderly man who works at the front desk, and promises to return it no later than the following Monday. That night, he reaches into the cloth pocket of his suitcase for the atlas of Great Britain he remembers asking Vasanti to place there. When he removes it, a piece of paper flutters to the ground. Vasanti has written out for him the inscription that Ramabai had long ago jotted on the first page of her prayer book. He reads it through: *It is no use asking why the small stream is not the mighty Ganges, or why the sparrow does not fan its feathers like the peacock, or why the coconut palm does not provide shade as does the banyan tree. Each is what it is and so it is with humankind: all His creation, we are what we are.*

All at once, the real meaning behind the inscription occurs to Baba. He realizes he now holds the answer to the one important and distressing aspect of Nanasahib's betrayal that he has been dodging: the question of the morality of a relationship that deviates from the norm. He knows the answer because Ramabai had figured it out, and had thought to write it down. Reading his mother's words again, the full extent of her compassion and tolerance dawns on him, and Baba's anger towards his father begins at last to lift.

~

It is a dull morning when Baba drives into Mr. Owens' village. He leaves his car at the bottom of the steep lane, and walks up the familiar path to the gate leading to the cottage. As he approaches, he is shocked to see Catherine through the window. He stops in his tracks. A closer look shows him that she is seated on the wooden horse. She is bucking it wildly, her chin pressed into her chest. Alarmed by her visibly unstable state and miserably nervous that he will now have to meet her, he almost retraces his steps. But if not anything else gratitude has to be expressed, the borrowed items have to be returned, and it would be an insult to the old man if Baba simply left them on the doorstep and walked away. Nevertheless, he hesitates a few moments before pressing the iron bell. The door opens right away. His aged benefactor stands there, shoulders sagging, a dead pipe sticking out of one side of his mouth, the furrows in his forehead unnaturally deep. Baba gives a tentative smile.

"Welcome back!" Mr. Owens says, his eyes widening in glad surprise.

His greeting is interrupted by a crash, and Baba follows Mr. Owens inside. Catherine has fallen to the floor, and her body is writhing awkwardly alongside the rocking horse. Mr. Owens crouches and touches her shoulder. Baba drops his duffle bag and together they lift Catherine's limp frame and place her on the cot. She is a pitiable sight: stiff as a board, stringy curls clinging to her forehead. Her eyes are half open and Baba nods a greeting before turning away.

Mr. Owens pulls up a blanket and covers his daughter's feet.

Baba follows his host to the metal hob, lowers his voice and says, "Apart from that one evening I had to restrain her, she wasn't as bad as this when I left."

"I was medicating her, wasn't I, all the time that you were here? She insisted she didn't want you to see her in her true condition."

Baba unbuttons his overcoat, his hands all at once shaking, and hangs it next to the cluster of walking sticks in the corner by the entrance. Mr. Owens stands in front of the fireplace and lights his pipe, his outstretched palm finding an anchor against the wall above the mantelpiece.

"Do sit down, Hari, and tell us everything," he says, glancing at Catherine, who is watching them both.

Baba takes a sip of the tea, and says, "My name is Vijay Chafékar."

"That's quite a mouthful—your name," Catherine says. "We shall continue to call you Hari, if you don't mind." Her voice is slurred and the pupils of her eyes are floating in crescents of white.

"By all means," Baba says. Swiftly searching her face to see if it holds any hint of what took place between them in the stone shelter so many weeks ago. But Catherine's expression is open, and betrays no awkwardness. Relieved, he describes everything that has happened since he left them: the recovery of his memory in a London hotel, retracing his steps to the Pinters', the Inner Temple with its bombed-out library and church, his studies and his decision to return home.

"Your invitation to visit," he says to Mr. Owens, "arrived at a point when I was ready to tear out my hair, I was so fed up with finding new ways to pass the time. Also, I wished to thank you for your generosity, for giving me shelter when you did. And I wanted to return all the items you so kindly loaned me."

Catherine is yawning. She closes her eyes and soon appears to be fast asleep.

Mr. Owens moves away from her cot and settles himself in the armchair. Baba tells him about his plan to drive to Harlech later that afternoon.

"You have a car?"

"I hired one."

"You do get around!" His host draws on his pipe with a thoughtful expression and as he puffs, the room comes alive with the sweet scent of tobacco.

"I have a favour to ask of you," Mr. Owens says at last. "It would mean postponing your visit to Harlech by a day, no more."

There is clutch inside Baba's stomach. "What can I do for you?"

"Catherine has an appointment at the Denbigh Asylum tomorrow. Do you think you could drive us there? I don't have to spell out to you the difficulty in taking her on the bus in her present condition."

Baba shudders at the thought of spending an extra day with Catherine, but he is indebted to Mr. Owens in more ways than one. "Of course," he says. "I'll drive you."

After checking to see whether Catherine is still sleeping—she is—Mr. Owens drops his voice. "About two or three years ago, much as I dislike going to London, I consulted a doctor there. He told me there is no medicine for her particular illness, no hope of recovery, no rehabilitation or cure. He warned that there would come a time when I would be unable to look after her. I sometimes wonder whether that day has arrived. Yet I'll never be ready to put her away. You've seen her when she's good. Why, even now, before she fell asleep, she was as normal as you and I."

His host's face is creased like an accordion, and Baba notices on the inner edge of Mr. Owens' left eyebrow a deep crest, deep enough to hold a drop of water or two. Once again he feels shaken with remorse for having given in to Catherine, who is even more vulnerable than he had thought at the time. Unbidden comes the memory of how she had clung to him in the hut on that disastrous day; the wild hair, the pale face, the green ribbon come undone, her lonely eyes yearning for closeness, validation, any intimacy that would dispel the gloomy darkness, if only for a minute.

Not wishing to postpone his apology a moment longer, Baba swallows. But as he readies himself to confess to Mr. Owens, he glances at Catherine. Her frozen eyes are fixed on him.

The words dry up in his throat.

~ EIGHTEEN ~

THE NEXT MORNING, there is frost on the ground when Baba and his hosts walk down the lane to the hired car. Catherine slides in behind the driver's seat and avoids meeting his eyes. A yellow head-scarf encircles her swollen face. Mr. Owens gets in beside him and Baba silently pulls out onto the road and drives away. He glances at Catherine now and again in the rear-view mirror, and when he looks at her this time, she points frantically towards the window and gasps at him to stop. He quickly does as requested, hops out, and opens her door. She hurries to the side of the road and heaves up her breakfast. When she turns around, her face wretched and streaked with water, Mr. Owens is standing by with a flask. She refuses the drink, and a few minutes later the car is on its way again. Catherine begins to sing, her words garbled by the strident wind that is pressing in through her rolled-down window. Baba glances at Mr. Owens, but the old man is staring ahead, poker-faced and tense.

Denbigh Asylum looks like a castle and is so imposing in the rolling, open countryside that Baba fleetingly wonders if Mr. Owens has mistakenly navigated them to the wrong address. But it is all too clear they have reached their destination when they pass a group of female inmates accompanied by two nurses. The young women are dressed in grey smocks, flat-bottomed shoes and stockings the colour of lead. One of them waves, displaying a toothy lopsided grin. Shaken by her unkempt hair and roving eye, Baba looks away and finds a spot to park the car. He locks the doors and follows Catherine and Mr. Owens, who are already entering the building. The matron leads them down a long winding corridor that opens into a small waiting room. An unseen person is softly laughing from behind a barred door.

The old man and Catherine are ushered in to see the doctor. Half an hour later, impatient to be on his way, Baba contemplates waiting for them in the car. But as he gets up to leave, the door behind him opens. Mr. Owens staggers out, looking haggard. A nurse follows on his heels and hands him a glass of water.

She stares coldly at Baba and says, "Are you the father?"

Perplexed, Baba points to Mr. Owens. The nurse makes a snorting sound and returns to the examination room.

After she has left, Baba turns to Mr. Owens. "What did the doctor say?"

"Catherine's not getting any better," he replies curtly, and Baba does not dare inquire further.

Shortly afterwards, Catherine enters the waiting room. The nurse admonishes her to look after herself before bidding her farewell.

Baba and his charges eat sandwiches while parked on the hillside overlooking the asylum. They take to the road again and Baba asks Mr. Owens how long he thinks it will take him to reach Harlech. Mr. Owens does not reply. His brooding silence feels so barbed that the journey appears long and tedious. Baba tries to divert himself by focusing on the countryside, on the autumnal gold that is beginning to spread its mantle on the rugged mountains, the honeystone cottages, the rolling hills.

It is early afternoon when Baba parks the car at the bottom of the hill beneath the cottage. Catherine has fallen asleep and he and Mr. Owens cannot get her to wake. "What'll we do?" he asks.

"We can't leave her here," Mr. Owens says.

"I'll carry her, then." Baba lifts Catherine out of the car. There are horse droppings in the lane and it seems as if he steps into every puddle, stubs the toe of his shoe on every stone, slips on slick, fallen leaves, all without once loosening his hold.

Inside the cottage, Mr. Owens points to the spare room. "You can lay her in there."

Baba eases Catherine onto the cot and the old man covers her body with a blanket. They leave quietly and Mr. Owens pulls shut the door behind him.

The packed lunch was meagre and Baba is hungry again. He amends his escape plan: he will stop at The Wild Pheasant for a quick bite before setting on his way. But first, there is that apology he owes his host. He draws a deep breath.

Before Baba can begin to speak, Mr. Owens asks, "Could you make up the fire?"

Baba sets about lighting it. The wood is slightly damp and by the time the flames are shooting up the chimney and throwing flickering shadows against the rounded hearth, Mr. Owens has made them both tea. He and Baba sit in adjacent armchairs and Baba wraps his hands around the mug for warmth, thinking that if he lingers too long before making an apology, Mr. Owens will strike up a conversation and he will not be able to leave. He takes one more sip, even though the tea is scalding, then firmly sets the mug down on the floor beside him.

"She's with child," Mr. Owens says.

Astounded by this unanticipated disclosure, Baba's chest contracts with dread.

"Catherine's with child," the old man repeats, without emotion.

And suddenly Baba recognizes the meaning behind the nurse's snappish question.

"Do you know who the father is?" he asks Mr. Owens, his skin crawling even as he suspects what the answer will be.

"She told us, the doctor and me, about what happened between you in August before you left." Mr. Owens' accusation is issued through clenched teeth. "You knew she was ailing. Yet you took advantage of her."

That's not the way it was, Baba wants to protest. *I was unwilling but she was wily and knew how to get her way.*

"I don't know how much Catherine confides in you," he says cautiously.

"What do you mean?"

"You must trust me when I tell you that I was not the first."

"That I know too well."

"Then how can you be so sure that the baby is mine?" His fingers trembling with sudden hope, Baba splays them on his knees.

Mr. Owens' voice loses its edge. "There were two, only two before you, if you must know. The first when Catherine was seventeen or so, the second when she was twenty-one. Both relationships lasted until the boys were wed—to other girls."

Baba instinctively knows the old man is telling the truth. He understands that Mr. Owens is a sensitive, watchful father who will do everything in his power to protect his daughter and whose sole purpose in life is to attend to her needs. All at once he remembers how uncomfortable Mr. Owens had been at the cottage that last Wednesday before Baba left, when Catherine was bashful and wreathed in smiles even as she baked her tarts filled with berries. Clearly, Mr. Owens had sensed his daughter's mood and was reluctant to leave the two of them together. But he'd had an appointment to keep, and Catherine was determined not to leave with him; and these minor details had decided Baba's fate.

He clears his throat several times and says, "In my defence, I wish to point out—please remember that I too was ill. Had I been in full control of my memory, I assure you I would never have done what I did. Personal circumstances would have prevented me." He speculates briefly whether he should tell Mr. Owens about Vasanti but decides against it; the timing is not right and the knowledge may further inflame the old man.

The neglected fire in the hearth has died down. The rocking horse appears petrified, its once glossy paint faded and peeling.

"All the way from Denbigh I kept telling myself that there has to be a solution," Mr. Owens says, poking at the ashes. He turns to Baba. "I don't think you should leave right away. Ride out the remaining seven or so months, and when you return to India, take the baby with you."

Baba gives a start and restrains himself from speaking out.

"You don't have to say it's yours. Say it is adopted. You have large families, I know. What's one extra mouth to feed?" Mr. Owens is speaking slowly, as though the idea expanding inside of him is taking root.

"That's simply not possible," Baba bursts out, his voice rising in protest. What if the baby looks like him? Would anyone accept his adoption story then? There would be a public scandal. And what effect would that have on Vasanti? On the verge again of imparting to Mr. Owens details about his family, Baba bites his tongue. The old man is clutching at straws, and knowing about Vasanti may provide him with added ammunition to drive home his point: take the baby to India and there will be a father *and* a mother to look after it.

"I can't do it," Baba says.

Mr. Owens slumps in his chair. "You need to give it more thought, Hari. You owe that to my daughter, to your unborn child, to us."

"I can't! You are asking too much of me. I'll send money and make sure that the child lacks for nothing." Now Baba is almost shouting.

Mr. Owens gets up with a jerk and his chair topples over. "Do you think I care about your money? Did you once hear me ask for money? If that's what I wanted, wouldn't I have said so? Hari, you must take the little one with you.

Who will look after it? My Cat? Me? Do you honestly think I have the energy to look after them both? And is not the baby your responsibility as well? How can you think of abandoning your flesh and blood?"

Mr. Owens' ferocious reminder resonates in Baba's gut. He flounders, unable to come up with an equitable rejoinder. If nothing else, he has learned from his own experience with Ramabai and Nanasahib that it is possible for suffering and differing parents to accept and adjust to each other without a breach of loyalty towards their children.

Now tears are gathering in Mr. Owens' eyes and his voice is strained with the effort it takes to keep himself from shouting, from waking Catherine in the adjacent room. "Have you forgotten the people inside her head? The malicious voices that tell her to do harm?" Mr. Owens moves towards Baba and now he is pleading. "Stay a while, Hari, I implore you. Then take the baby and give it the life it deserves."

"No!" Catherine's voice is firm and filled with desperation.

Baba and Mr. Owens spin around. Catherine is standing in the doorway, her lips a livid gash in her drawn face.

The two men look at each other; how much has she heard?

Catherine's hunched body is sliding down the wall. Her scarf is askew and has tightened around her neck; her eyes are wide. "No one is going to take my baby away from me.

Not Hari, not you, not the doctors, or the nurses. Do you understand me, Pappy? No. One."

"Pet." Mr. Owens kneels in front of her and, searching her eyes, his hands are shaking but his voice is cajoling and calm. "Allow us to at least consider the possibility of Hari looking after the little one. He is equally responsible for the unborn child, don't you think? After all, he is its father. Hmm?" All at once he turns around and Baba can sense a new idea taking form inside Mr. Owens' head. "What if you take Catherine with you?" he says quickly. "Adopt them both."

Baba steps back in horror.

But Mr. Owens immediately clenches his right fist and smacks his mouth in remorse. "No, no, Catherine love, what was I thinking? You'll miss me and your piano and these hallowed hills. And whatever will I do without you?"

"Do you know how difficult it is, Pappy, for me to know what is real and unreal? And here you are, making plans to snatch away the only real thing I might ever have." Catherine runs her hand over a belly that is as yet level and flat.

Tears are running down Mr. Owens' cheeks; he wipes them with his palms. "I know how much you suffer, pet. All I want is for the baby to have a decent future."

"I cannot give it up. Don't you see? Think how the voices will chastise me then. It was their idea. More *hers* than theirs. *She* instructed me on how to go about it. And her plan worked, did it not?"

Mr. Owens looks over at Baba in shock.

Baba, too, is horrified by Catherine's disturbing admission, and for a moment he wishes he were dead. He curses himself for not understanding that when Catherine had dawdled over her chores and tied that satin ribbon around her hair, she had been getting ready to put into action her deranged scheme. And he had gone along with it, had allowed her to persuade him to accompany her to Eileen's, and in the hut when she had made her move, he had readily presumed she understood that he would be leaving forever the following day.

He straightens Mr. Owens's toppled chair and slumps into it, clutching his hair. He recalls how, on the ship from Bombay to Liverpool, he had gone over and over what he would do if the Germans refocused their attention on London, where he would go, the measures he would take. Yet how could he have anticipated this? He leans forward and disturbs the ashes with the poker until the fireplace fills with black cloud.

"Hari? You wish to return to India?" Mr. Owens is saying, his voice formal now. He removes the poker from Baba's hand and places it out of his reach. "Return then. Between Catherine and I, we will raise the little one. We've managed before and we'll manage again."

Baba raises his eyes. Catherine is still crouched beside the wall, her forehead almost touching the floor.

"It's getting late, and you want to reach Harlech in good time, do you not?" Mr. Owens holds out Baba's overcoat. His expression is wistful. He says, "When you first came here, I used to think: wouldn't it be brilliant if our Hari never regained his memory and made his home with us? For right from that first day we met you, you were such a gentleman, treating my Cat as though her illness did not matter . . . Get going now, and if you care to send me your address, I will keep you informed."

Baba shrugs into his coat, opens the cottage door, and without a backward glance steps out into an afternoon filled with long shadows.

~ NINETEEN ~

SINGLE SHEEP ON THE hillside is bleating despondently, as though lost. Baba walks down the lane and slips into his car. Mr. Owens' cottage is somewhere above him, hidden from sight. The valley at his feet is stippled with patches of dying sunlight, and light mists wreathe the craggy walls of the mountains. He turns on the ignition, then switches it off.

He does not want to visit Harlech, not any more. What he wants—so strongly that he can hardly breathe for the longing—is to bury his face in Vasanti's lap. It is a stroke of luck, he tells himself firmly, that Mr. Owens is able to accept the truth regarding his daughter: that it is *she* who tricked him, the amnesiac, into falling in with her design. Assuring him that father and daughter will look after the

unborn child is surely Mr. Owens' way of acknowledging
that Baba is not to blame.

Yet, despite Mr. Owens' generosity of spirit and assur-
ances, uncomfortable questions burrow into Baba's mind.
What if Catherine's unfortunate mental condition continues to worsen during her confinement? Will Mr. Owens be
able to manage her? What if she has to be institutionalized?
Will the baby be born in a mental asylum? And will it, in
the absence of a father and because Catherine is not willing
to part with it and Mr. Owens too feeble to care for it, grow
up in an institution for the insane? He briefly imagines a
child fondled, scolded and raised by a family of scowling
inmates. If he leaves right now, this very minute, and sails
on the ship to Bombay, never to return, will he really be
spared the consequences of his decision? What about his
guilt-ridden thoughts? Will ignorance about what is happening to his child confer on him peace, that essential ingre-
dient to starting afresh? And even if he were to pretend
that all was well, would Vasanti remain insensible to the
fact that something was terribly wrong deep within him?
Would she rest until she had extracted from him the sordid,
shameful truth?

And yet, if he were to remain here for the sake of his
hapless child, what would become of his beloved wife?

Restlessly, Baba reaches for the atlas in the seat pocket
next to him. As he flips through its pages, he comes across

the note that had tumbled to the floor in his Liverpool hotel room: his mother's inscription, the one that was written on the first page of her prayer book, then copied by Vasanti onto a piece of a paper and inserted between the pages where he would be sure to find it. His fingertips lose their warmth as he recalls the morning when he had first read Ramabai's dedication, at the guesthouse in Chikaldhara, hours after their mother had passed away. He remembers his last evening together when Ramabai had talked about how important it had been for her and Nanasahib to work towards building a future for their offspring; how necessary it was for parents to support each child's endeavours; and how parents must compromise so as not to adversely affect their children's well-being. Baba recalls the promise she had obtained from him that night—one that, in his youthful way and filled with love for his mother, he had readily given: never to abandon his own children, no matter the circumstances.

Perhaps his current complication is destiny's strange way of making him keep his promise *and* returning him to London, he thinks. Perhaps he is meant to resume his interrupted efforts at being called to the bar, after all. And despite himself, the idea that has for so long lingered inside him, that of one day becoming a barrister, brings a twisted smile to his lips. Yes, this is what he must do, what he *will* do. Instead of sailing on the *Eastern Star* he will go back to his studies and await the birth of his child in London. And after that—well, he remembers hearing that giving birth alters the state and status of a woman. Perhaps Catherine will get better. The sight of her baby will surely encourage her to devote her thoughts and energies to this child she has gone to such great lengths to acquire. But even as this ray of optimism breaks through his unpromising thoughts, he knows that any weak hope he has is based on a house of cards. He has seen Catherine at her worst. Without any promise of medication to make her better, it is doubtful that she will ever come out of her illness in a meaningful way.

He wishes now that he had taken his uncle and mentor, Bhikumama, into his confidence and told him the real reason why he was running away from home. No doubt Bhikumama would never have given his blessing to Baba's scheme had he known the truth. He thinks sorrowfully about his brothers, too; if he had shared with them what he had seen on that revelatory afternoon in Pegasus, they surely would have done their best to talk him out of the anger and feeling of betrayal that had caused him to turn his back on Nanasahib, and in doing so calmed the destructive sentiment that had—however indirectly—jeopardized the mental peace not only of Vasanti all of Chafékar Wadi. Baba's aloofness and the groundless animosity he had felt towards his brothers had cost him dearly. As he continues to analyze and dissect various aspects of the distressing situation, Baba's mind curls away from the painful irony that his self-condemnation is the result of Bhikumama having taught him so well the importance of being scrupulously honest and weighing an issue from every angle.

Gazing at the single silhouette of a spiky gnarled tree with grey bark and red berries growing sideways out of the slope to the right and front of him, Baba's thoughts return to his unborn child. A certain tenderness for the innocent life that is yet a minuscule kernel rises unbidden. He tries to stay in that gentle moment, but the repetitive questions inside his head will not allow him to rest for long. With Catherine's condition worsening, will Mr. Owens, a grandfather, alone and unsupported, be able to fill the shoes of a mother and a father? He has never met Catherine's cousin Eileen; can she be counted upon to help?

His mind turns to Christopher, and again Baba wishes he could confide in his old friend. Yet now more than ever it is imperative that Christopher, because of his connection to Chafékar Wadi, not know the truth, lest it escape his lips and reach the ears of Susan or their father, and in turn be leaked to Baba's family. Baba reflects how it is just as well that his letter to Vasanti, along with his raincoat, was lost on that fatal day on Mount Snowdon—for it was the only letter he had written during his time in London that contained Mrs. Pinter's address.

Yes, Baba thinks firmly, it is decided: he will return to London.

And once back in London, for the year or two it takes to complete his studies he will take up other lodgings, far less costly than Mrs. Pinter's. He will conserve his funds to the best of his ability. Swallowing the dryness in his throat, he forces himself to think even further ahead; one day, if indeed circumstances—the birth of his child, concern for the infant's welfare—make it impossible for him to return to Chafékar Wadi, it will be necessary for him to leave this small island. He mulls over the possibilities of where in the world he might go so that he and his child would remain untraceable, and all at once it comes to him: he will travel west across the ocean and make their new home somewhere in the vast, remote beauty of the Alberta prairies he has so recently heard about.

Baba sits hunched in his car at the foot of Mr. Owens' steep icy lane, petrified to the core of his being, the sky slowly darkening to night, and imagines over and over again Vasanti's desolation should he never return. Through the long hours he curses and blames himself for the shock and sadness that would take hold of Chafékar Wadi then. But it is the impact of his decisions on Vasanti that haunts him, keeps him in a state of anguished fear, full of dread for her unhappiness, horror for her widowed state. And as the sky slides into grey dawn, Baba realizes that amongst all this uncertainty, one thing *is* certain: If and when he is required to disappear from the face of the Earth, he must do it in such a way that Vasanti will renounce all hope and not forever await his return.

September 16, 1944

Dearest, darling Baba,

You cannot be dead. You are *not* dead! The telegram from
your landlady arrived fourteen days ago, followed by her
letter only this morning informing us of the details: that
you met your death after falling off the side of a mountain
in the Scottish Highlands while on a walking expedition.
Why were you in Scotland? What mountain? What expedition? No, you are in London, and you are alive. Would I
not sense, feel, experience your loss if indeed you were no
more? So, where are you? And who is this landlady, this
"Dorothy Tipton?" It is almost two years since you sent us
your permanent address and during all this time I imagined the person behind *c/o Mrs. Tipton* to be a grey-haired,
elderly lady. Now, after reading the letter, I'm not so sure.

I regret I did not write to you before. If only I wasn't
such a proud and mulish fool. Oh, the number of letters I

finished but did not post because of what I said when you left India, about writing only if you wrote me first. Why *didn't* you write to me? How to describe the anger I have felt at your continued silence, the endless sense of betrayal, the drowning hurt. Day in, day out for more than two years I waited for the postman, sometimes walking to the front gate to intercept him there. There was never anything from you, not even a postcard. Just the occasional letter addressed to Nanasahib that you were well and busy with your studies, and we were not to worry if there was a long gap in communication. And then this bombshell telegram from your landlady followed by an even more baffling explanation of your demise.

"A great tumultuous change would visit you in your twenty-fifth year," isn't that what the misshapen man predicted in the cottage when you were fourteen years old? "No death," he said, "only turbulence and turmoil." So whatever trouble you are in, Baba, whatever catastrophe may have befallen you, it doesn't matter just so long as you are alive. I entreat you, please, please let us know the nature of your difficulty and allow your father and brothers to find a solution, as I know they will. Yogesh wants to travel to England to bring back your ashes but Nanasahib will not permit him, especially now that the bombs are once again falling on London.

Chafékar Wadi has lost its sheen. The cooks cook but

nobody eats. People have been dropping by hour after hour and your father meets them all with stooped shoulders and vacant eyes. Within a week of receiving the telegram, despite everyone in the family advising him to the contrary, Nanasahib called a friend and sold him Pegasus right there and then. Much as it hurts to convey this to you, your father's grief is difficult to bear; I avoid him whenever I can. Mr. Watson has been given notice to vacate his lodgings because Nanasahib intends to live there. Sheelatai has been pleading that he will be much better off in the main house. But your father, as stubborn as you, refuses to listen to anything anyone says. "I need my solitude," he repeats. I long to tell him that you are not dead but I cannot plant that idea without any proof. It would be too cruel of me to give him hope.

So, give me that proof, Baba, give me hope. Write me a letter—better still, come back home.

In the meantime, I have no choice but to let the rest of them grieve. As for me, I continue to await your return, and now that you are finished your studies I trust that you will be back with us before long; pale, thin, perhaps walking with a slight limp as a result of your *almost* fatal fall in the Scottish Highlands. You will appear at our bedroom door without warning, the rest of the family banked behind you, their faces wet with amazed joy. You will flash me a wink and I will remain transfixed, leaning against the bed for support, not daring to devour you with my eyes in the presence of Nanasahib. He will come forward and placing his hands on your shoulders, give you a gentle push.

But, until that day, I will keep writing to you, my dearest, my love, my beloved, and live in the constant hope that I will see you again soon at Chafékar Wadi.

Yours forever,

Vasanti

ACKNOWLEDGEMENTS

For help in bringing this book to life, many thanks to my editor at Doubleday Canada, Lynn Henry; thanks also to Martha Kanya-Forstner. My gratitude to my agent, Dean Cooke, for standing by me through the long years.

Any historical inaccuracies regarding World War II are mine.

I wish to acknowledge the timely support of the Canada Council for the Arts and the Banff Centre's Wired Writing Studio.